ELEPHANT IN THE LIVING ROOM

The story of a skateboarder, a
missing dog and a family secret

BY

ALISON LESLIE GOLD

AND

DARIN ELLIOTT

TMI Publishing, Providence, RI
www.tmipublishing.com

Elephant in the Living Room

Second edition
ISBN: 978-1-938371-25-7
TMI Publishing, Providence, RI

First Edition:
Oneiro Press Edition, UK
ISBN-13: 978-1500833091

Author's website: www.AlisonLeslieGold.com
www.facebook.com/AlisonLeslieGold
www.facebook.com/DarinElliott

TMI Publishing
61 Doyle Avenue
Providence, RI 02906
www.tmipublishing.com

TABLE OF CONTENTS

BECKETT'S PROLOGUE

While I sit here in a cage among dozens of other dogs (and even some cats - yuck, gross!) let me introduce myself. My name is Beckett and I belong to Danielle Godot and her family.

Or rather, I did.

Danielle, age eleven and three-quarters, rescued me from the County Shelter for Abandoned and Battered Animals two years ago. Although I only have one and a half ears, she still swooped down on me and brought her face close to mine and kissed my snout.

(Half of my right ear, my best one, got frostbitten and snapped off when I was abandoned up on snowy Big Elk Mountain by my first owner who lost his job. In those days my name was - please keep it to yourself - Bobolina. But that's another story for another time.)

Regardless of my unsightly ear, and that I'm a cross between a Terrier, a Cocker Spaniel and some unknown Poodle-trash - what you humans call a mongrel, but what we dogs consider A Unique Blend - Danielle picked ME rather than a too cute Yorkie named Vladimir who also vied for her attention.

She took me home and very quickly I became a crucial member of the Godot family.

Danielle gave me my name because she knew of an Irish writer named Samuel Beckett, who wrote a story about someone waiting for a dude named Godot. She told me that I looked like I had been waiting a long time for someone. And even though that writer was a HE and I am a SHE, it never occurred to Danielle that it mattered, so it doesn't to me, either. I mean, hey, it's a lot better than Bobolina!

Almost every evening Danielle and her younger brother Simon, who is eight and one-third, would argue over which of them would have me in their room for the night. Though their mother, Minnie, made an official rule that they had to take turns with me, more often than not, even if it wasn't her night Danielle won out. She was very good at getting her way.

So because I spent all that time with her, and she took the best care of me, I guess you could say I felt closest to her. And she felt the same about me, obviously. I mean, when the Godots had liver or Brussels sprouts for dinner, Danielle ALWAYS secretly passed hers under the table to me. Now that's love! Funny food for a dog, but you won't hear me complaining - I'll eat just about anything! Except mushrooms. Blech! And even when I did something doggish, like chewing her favorite sneakers or leaving claw marks all over her homework papers, and she would scowl at me and grunt, I knew she didn't hold it against me.

I'm not the only pet in the Godot family, mind you. No such luck! They also have a green parakeet who stares and squawks a lot and a fluffy black rabbit who poops non-stop. While I lived there, those two didn't seem to mind my STARRING role, and even liked me sometimes, though neither one ever wanted me to get too affectionate, especially after I chased the rabbit in the back yard so quickly that she fell into Minnie's Japanese pond. Man, she stunk like goldfish for a week!

So I, Beckett, was Número Uno. Until disaster struck. You see, sixteen days ago, Danielle's dad, Sam (a big, sporty guy who's not in great shape like he used to be), took me to a new dog park that was quite far from our home. While I was off dashing around with Penelope the Pit Bull and Ruby the Ger-

man Shepherd, Sam went off to a beach party reunion with his Army buddies.

He must have gulped down too many beers because he forgot all about me, and then … it hurts to even say it … he never came back to get me!

Or, if he did, it wasn't until after dark, after a rainstorm, after the dog park was locked for the night, after I was forced to hit the road and try to find my way home. Before long I was ravenous and there was no food around. None! Nada!

To be honest, it's not the first time Sam forgot about me – many times he went off for a walk with the leash but no Me on the end, and once he left me alone in the car for hours while he hung out in a dingy bar. His behavior was starting to worry me and then that Most Terrible of Days occurred and I ended up here.

For two weeks I have been in this animal shelter, trapped, bored, longing for a cuddle. Waiting … yes, waiting, like in that Irish writer's story.

Meanwhile, there is another story about the Godot family that needs telling. It's about a family secret that nobody wants to discuss, and involves my disappearance and doesn't. And it is continuing on right now, every day, while I'm far away, missing them all, even that half-witted parakeet.

Do lend me your ears or, at least, half an ear, while it's being told.

And forgive me if every once in a while I insert my two cents into the story, since sometimes humans don't tell the WHOLE truth, or think the way we dogs can!

PART ONE

THE INVISIBLE ELEPHANT

CHAPTER 1

If the moon happens to be bright, it shines into the Godot family's kitchen window, casting a bone-blue light across the kitchen table that's got four placemats on it. Each placemat is made from a photo of Beckett, the family's recently lost dog.

(This is me, Beckett, and please note: Danielle chose ME to get encased in plastic and not that dumb parakeet or dumber rabbit, so it is my face (FOUR of them!) that gazes up lovingly at each Godot at mealtimes.)

But tonight there's no moon, so the kitchen is pitch black. The first hints of autumn are in the air, and all is silent except for an occasional drop of water falling with an eerie plop from the drippy spigot into the kitchen sink. Someone has forgotten to cover Pickle's cage. Pickle is a green parakeet. He eats mosquitoes, ants, almost any bug, though his usual food is millet and bird seed. He is a Buddhist, and also a Virgo.

The Godot kids, besides giving their pets a name, also assign each one an astrological sign and its own religion. They considered Beckett a Sagittarian because they adopted her on December 15th. And she's a Unitarian since her shelter was across the street from a Unitarian Church.

(Crazy. We dogs don't get your People Religions. Our religion is Eat, Pee, Poop, Sleep, Chase Things and Try Always to Get Cuddles. What more could anybody want?)

Pickle's cage hangs on a metal hook beside the kitchen table. From there he sees everything that goes on and he's usually alert. This night he stares down as a pair of hands appears out of the shadows. Concealed in green gardening gloves, the hands line up sharp knives on the table. His pinpoint eyes watch as the gloves pick up a knife and begin winding silver duct tape round and round its pointy glinting blade.

The gloved hands do the same thing to the rest of the dangerous knives - one by one. Pickle has good night vision, but the dark is impenetrable, hiding the identity of the person wearing the gloves.

Pickle shakes his head, fluffing his feathers - he is a little creeped out by what he's not seeing.

Then, startling Pickle and causing the garden gloves to pause in mid-air, the song "Without Me" by the rapper Eminem blasts out from somewhere in the house. Hastily the gloved hands gather up the knives and drop them back into their drawer with a clattering noise, slamming it shut. The gloved hands and the shadowy person wearing them quickly vanish into the darkness.

Abruptly "Without Me" stops playing.

There is silence except for that water. Plop. Plop.

Then something crashes inside the house.

Pickle blinks his eyes a few times and squawks.

CHAPTER 2

Even more loudly, "Without Me" starts up again. The drum beats are making the walls vibrate.

Upstairs, jolted out of a deep sleep, Flopsie, the Jewish Capricorn rabbit, darts off through the open door of her cage with un-rabbitish speed. At the top of the stairway she bumps into Danielle's rigid legs, attached to Danielle, of course.

(That's Flopsie for you. I told you she was dippy.)

Danielle's wearing purple striped pajamas, her auburn hair is a tangled mess because she refuses to have it cut or combed until she's reunited with her lost dog. She bends down and lifts Flopsie up and carries her to the door of Simon's bedroom.

She sees her little brother sitting up in the lower bunk. The jarring music has woken him too. He's got long legs, nutmeg-colored hair and has a few freckles across his nose.

(Actually, his hair is the exact color of my kibbles. He liked me, too, and used to tickle my furry tummy and buy me chewy bones with money from his allowance.)

When he notices Danielle standing tensely at the door, with Flopsie in her white-knuckled hands, Simon jumps up and grabs the rabbit. He cradles the trembling animal against the top of his Star Wars pajamas while he pets her soft head. He's a worrier, and knows that Flopsie is delicate. He wants to comfort his big sister, too, but doesn't know what he can say that might help because she's become so prickly since Beckett's disappearance.

The music abruptly stops. The house is as silent as a hole in the ground: a very deep hole, and one that Danielle is afraid she is about to fall into. Suddenly the music starts again and a fearful feeling returns.

"Don't just stand there, Dani," Simon whispers. "Come in." She sits at the foot of his bunk, drawing her knees up to her chest. The loud music that is invading the quiet peace of night seems even creepier than before.

Danielle complains, "At least last week it was only the Bee Gees. But rap. Grow up, Dad!"

"Yeah, and another meal with wine. Don't they know how much their wine stinks?"

"And how goofy he gets?" Danielle rolls her eyes.

"My friend Jerry's dad is a doctor, and he says that one glass a day is good for you," Simon adds.

"I know Jerry's dad is a doctor. I hate it when people tell me things I already know. I wish Dad drank only one glass, but with him it's usually three or four."

"Or five!" Simon adds. "What's wrong with diet Pepsi? That's what Jerry's dad drinks after dinner."

"Oh, yuck. Diet Pepsi tastes like … like smoked pee."

"Not to me!" Simon snaps back, setting Flopsie down beside him, of course not knowing what smoked pea tastes like.

"I asked Mom to bring home some soda and juice instead of all that stinky stuff," Simon tells her. "She said she would but she didn't."

"She forgot Flopsie's peeled organic carrots, too," Danielle adds. "And Dad forgot Open School Night last week. No one in this family can remember anything anymore. I think we're in a family of forgetters. I hope I didn't inherit THAT gene!"

"Danielle," Simon asks with curiosity, "why does wine smell so disgusting?"

"Maybe it's the fermentation."

"What's for-man-tation?"

"Sometimes you're such a dork. Wine is made from grape juice, and fermentation is when they, like, add bacteria or something and it goes all stinky."

"Hmm," Simon replies, stroking Flopsie's long ears.

"Hey, aren't YOU forgetting something?"

"What?"

"It's my night to sleep with Flopsie! Give her back."

Simon hands over the rabbit.

"I'd let you have her," Danielle adds, softening her voice, "but I'm missing Beckett really bad tonight. I keep smelling her on my blanket."

"That's okay, I won't miss those little black turds Flopsie leaves in my sheets that get stuck between my toes."

"Yeah, I know. I call them pell-pell, 'cuz they're like pellets."

"What? You named her poo?" Simon asks, scrunching his nose.

"It's not a name, it's a description. Like Pickle goes plip-plop, 'cuz that's what birds do, and fish go string-string and when a cat goes it's like they're squeezing toothpaste out of a tube."

"And dogs? What do you call their poo?"

"I'll tell you when you're older," Danielle replies and leaves.

Back in her own bedroom, Danielle doesn't get into bed but stands at the window and looks outside at the moonless street.

(Of course, she's wondering where I am. If only she knew that right now I'm in a shelter in Vista Hill and haven't been washed in two weeks. I miss her too, even the baths she used to give me with the garden hose. I hated them then but would run a mile for one now.)

Beside the window, the lemon-yellow walls of Danielle's room are covered with photos of Flopsie, of Pickle and, most frequently and in absentia, of Beckett - some flattering, some not.

(I wish she had found a way to photograph me that didn't show my half-ear!)

Again and again, the harsh music punctures the serenity of the night. Danielle jumps into bed, draws Flopsie near her and pulls the covers up over her face. Then, grabbing a long sprig of scraggily hair on either side of her head, twists and scrunches each into an ear to try and block out the noise.

It just about works - the sound is muffled now. Then she gets a whiff of Beckett's unique smell still lingering on her blanket and takes a deep breath. This helps her to finally fall asleep.

But not Flopsie who is wide awake, her nose twitching to the rap beat.

CHAPTER 3

With a green skateboard under her arm, Danielle leaves the house the next morning and walks up the street.

(This is the skateboard on which she'd sometimes carry me under her arm while riding. It always scared me a little, especially when she'd jump the curb and my butt would bounce.)

Her books and lunch are in the blue and black backpack on which a photo of Beckett has been glued. Above the photo are words written in big bold letters:

HAVE YOU SEEN THIS VERY COOL, VERY CUTE DOG?

(I'm impressed. But she could have added "CLEVER" too!)

The elderly neighbor, Mrs. Harper, is on the sidewalk out front with her three large Dobermans. Her gray-white hair is a jumble, and she's wearing the faded floral bathrobe that she never seems to take off. Danielle greets her and reaches down to pet the dogs. Sadly, Mrs. Harper is getting on in years and can no longer remember the names of her dogs. The nephew who helped move her into her house a few years earlier hasn't visited in a long time, so there's been no one to ask what the dogs are called. Not to hurt Mrs. Harper's feelings, people have stopped asking. They are known simply as the Three Nameless Dobermans.

It was Danielle who came up with that title one afternoon with her best friend, Nicky, while up in the tree-house that her father built out back in a big old oak tree. They used to spend lots of time up there, playing board games or cards, and often carried snacks or lunches up on weekends. Sometimes they even hoisted Beckett up in a basket.

(Ok, did I love that? No! Even dogs get motion-sick.)

One time they tried to spend the night in the tree-house. They brought up sleeping bags and flashlights and a whistle in case of an emergency or squirrel attack, but got spooked and climbed down after an hour and slept on the porch instead.

They even made a special trap door that swings on hinges and locks to keep unwanted guests (Simon, mostly) from getting in. From up there they could spy on Mrs. Harper in her back yard, or see into her kitchen window to check what she is watching on TV. For example, they know that she watches "The Dog Whisperer." Even so, Mrs. Harper doesn't seem to have a clue about how to train dogs. Right now they're yanking on their leashes, almost pulling her over.

Danielle leans in further to hug them one by one. She strokes their soft ears and bends down to sniff them.

(That she is hugging one dog, two dogs, then a third, that are NOT me, makes me more than a little jealous. But dog ears, she often said, are her second favorite smell after fresh baked bread. My one and a half included! See, I told you - Danielle's a dog-lover!)

She stands up and tells Mrs. Harper, "Anytime you want me to -." Remembering that Mrs. Harper is nearly deaf, she shouts, "Anytime You Want Me To Walk Them, I'll Be Glad To, Okay? I'll Even Take Them For A Run In The Dog Park."

"That would be very nice, dear. They could use a run. As you can see, I'm not much into running these days. Just come by anytime, anytime …"

The dogs pull Mrs. Harper down the street, her floral bathrobe flapping at the bottom.

Danielle gets on her skateboard and skates away, looking back a few times at the Dobermans with concern. Normally she would head west down Scutter Lane to get to school, but this morning she goes in the opposite direction.

Seven or eight streets away, in a desolate part of town, is one of the town's busiest dog parks. When she gets there, she does a perfect heel-flip, then jumps off the skateboard and slides it under her arm. She stands at the fence and carefully surveys all the dogs that are frolicking in the park.

(Once again I'm not among them. And once again her heart must ache. As does mine.)

Now there's nothing left but to go to school, and she'd better hurry. She zooms along in the street beside passing cars. It may seem dangerous, but Danielle's been riding that skateboard since she got it on her sixth birthday. Because she practices almost every day, she's a mini-expert. Even better than her best friend Nicky, although he is quickly catching up.

CHAPTER 4

On Friday, after school has let out for the day, Danielle carries a stack of signs and a roll of tape as she skates quickly along Main Street wearing her favorite red hoodie. Alongside her, also on a skateboard, rolls Nicky in a Spiderman T-shirt. His brown hair has recently been clipped close to his scalp. He has alert green eyes and a slender face. They have been best friends so long now that they can often tell what the other is thinking without having to speak; sometimes they burst out laughing at the same moment and people think they're a little nutty. And they both like pepperoni pizza, fizzy lemonade, "The Simpsons," card games, reading, the color red, and, most of all, skateboarding and dogs.

(Please note!!)

They stop at every corner so that Danielle can stand on her skateboard and tape a sign onto a utility pole while Nicky balances on his and holds the sign in place.

The sign reads:

LOST DOG WITH HALF AN EAR MISSING
TERRIER AND SPANIEL MIX
SIGN: SAGITTARIUS,
RELIGION: UNITARIAN
ANSWERS TO THE NAME BECKETT
NOT A PICKY EATER -
EATS ALMOST ANYTHING, ANYTIME
(EXCEPT MUSHROOMS)

At the bottom of the sign is a home phone number, an e-mail address and an SMS number.

(If only Danielle knew how skimpy last night's plate of dry food was despite the good intentions of the people at the shelter I'm at. I mean, my ribs are sticking out! I'd even be thankful for the ginger snaps she used to offer that I would spit out when she wasn't looking.)

Where they live -

(Where I used to live, too!)

- is a small town rising up on tiered streets above the blue Pacific Ocean. At almost any time, surfers in black rubber wetsuits, looking like aliens from outer space, are either riding a wave or lying face down on their surfboards waiting for one to roll in.

Below them is the inviting Limerick Beach Pier, jutting out over the sandy beach and the sea.

Danielle and Nicky jump off and carry their skateboards up a steep hill. They've finished plastering the town center with their signs.

(It's very kind of them, but it's not my best photo - I don't mean to sound vain but one of my eyes looks slanted and there's some drool on my lower lip.)

"Hey, Dani, good news!" Nicky announces. "My parents have finally agreed to let me have a dog. Maybe two, since one dog could keep the other company while they're at work and I'm at school."

"Cool," Danielle responds, with less enthusiasm than he had hoped for.

Nicky notices Beckett's face staring at him from the photo on her backpack and regrets that he didn't wait for a better moment to mention it.

Soon they reach Nicky's bright green house on Rosemary Street. He slams his foot down on the front of his skateboard, it flips up and he catches it mid-air, smiling.

"You've been practicing your kick-flip," Danielle comments, impressed, giving him a thumbs up.

"Yeah. Now I'm gonna work on the varial kick-flip and whip your butt at the skateboard park next weekend."

He turns towards the door, then back to her.

"Hey, maybe you could stay over this weekend?"

Danielle doesn't reply.

"Don't you want to hang out here, anymore?" He throws a fake punch to her shoulder. "You always used to, now you hardly ever do."

"I know," she mumbles.

"Why?"

"What if Beckett found her way home and I wasn't there?"

"That's true. Well, maybe another weekend then. Think about it."

"Okay."

"See ya at school tomorrow."

His house key is on a string around his neck. He turns the key in the lock as Danielle looks back and smiles at him - her old smile. She gets back on her skateboard and shoots away.

Soon she turns a corner and rolls onto her street, jumping the curb near her house and doing an ollie. Then, pushing her luck, she does a nollie, which she messes up, nearly crashing down onto the sidewalk.

Instead of going home, Danielle slips her skateboard under her arm and knocks at Mrs. Harper's door. There's no answer. She walks along the side of the house and arrives at the gate to the back yard. Opening the gate, she tentatively steps in.

Immediately she's hit by an awful smell and grabs her nose. The yard is overgrown with eucalyptus trees that have shed leaves and whole branches. And everywhere the ground is dotted with dog poo – some fresh and baking in the sun, some old and already mixing in with the weeds and dirt.

She finds a path, and carefully - to avoid stepping in poo - makes her way along it until she reaches Mrs. Harper's kitchen door. Then she loudly knocks.

As soon as Mrs. Harper cracks open the door, the dogs push past her. They gather around, sniffing and leaning their heads forward.

"Can I take them for a walk?" Danielle asks.

"I remember that hood, but not you. Remind me who you are, please," Mrs. Harper says. "And talk louder."

"What HOOD?" Danielle wonders, raising her voice.

"Hood. You're wearing a hood. Like Robin Hood."

"Oh, my hoodie," she giggles, flopping it up and down off her head. "I'm Danielle. I live next door. DAN-NEE, remember?"

Mrs. Harper is still uncertain, but points at the doorknob, "Their leashes!"

Danielle hooks a leather leash to the collar of each large dog. She puts her backpack on top of her skateboard and stacks both at the side of the room.

"Can I leave these here?"

"Of course," Mrs. Harper answers, eyeing the skateboard with curiosity, "whatever THAT is. Just please bring them back, Robin Hood."

The Dobermans are strong and drag her through the gate to the sidewalk. With all three of them united as one in pulling her, she is reminded of "The Three Musketeers" book she read last summer.

"All for One and One for Aaaaalllllllll!!!" she shouts as they take off in a blast of energy hurrying her down the street.

The nearby dog park where they're headed is divided into a section for small dogs and a larger section for big dogs. She releases them into the larger section, where they happily leap and dash and romp with other dogs inside.

Quickly, she begins scanning the small dog section, on the lookout for Beckett.

(Oh, how happy we would both be if I were there!!! But I'm not. I am lying on a cold cement floor counting the ants that march past. Bo - ring!)

She picks a stick off the ground, looks around at the dogs until she spots a white Poodle with pink bows tied on each ear. Then Danielle waves the stick at the Poodle while reciting what sounds like a convincing magic spell - "Petralis obli-changio." If only she had the power to change the dog into Beckett, she thinks as she drops the stick.

(Thankfully she does not. I have enough Pooble in my genes as it is! That glitzy Poodle at the park stays the glitzy Poodle and I stay me, far, far away and bereft. Maybe Dani used the wrong spell.)

CHAPTER 4½

Okay, it's time for me, Beckett, to interrupt and dedicate a chapter (or at least half of one) to MY adventures after Sam left me in the park that Most Terrible of Days.

When it happened, I was off peeing a few drops on a tree trunk saturated with lots of dog-pee smells. (That's why we do it, in case you didn't know. It's not just to "leave our mark", as you humans claim, but to join the Great Community of Dogs by intermixing our pee on a tree. True.)

Usually I run back after a pee session and Sam's talking to some other dog owner or gabbing on his cell-phone, but on that Most Terrible of Days, I got back to where I'd left him and he was nowhere to be seen, or smelled. At first I thought, "Well, Beckett, you just ran back to the wrong spot." So I zigzagged all over the park, and then did it again. And then AGAIN! No Sam!!

Now let me explain something else about dogs you might not know. We are totally, absolutely, thoroughly, megananamously (I made that word up) devoted to our masters. Well, "master" is YOUR word for yourselves. We dogs call you our Tall Tailless Two-legged Carers.

But we are DE-VOT-ED. We want to be around you guys all the time. That's why we follow you into every room, the front yard, the back yard, the garage and even the bathroom. So going to our "master" and not finding him or her is truly AWFUL. We freak out.

Once we have the luck to have a master, we don't know how to be a Dog-without-Master anymore. Yes, maybe a million years ago we roamed around with other dogs – I mean wolves

– *what you guys call a "pack," but it's not a million years ago. I mean, there were no Cocker Spaniels or Poodles running around in caveman times.*

So after realizing that Sam was NOT in the park, that he had LEFT and NOT taken ME, my heart cracked. When I recovered, I set off trying to get home.

ANOTHER DOG MYTH: That we can ALWAYS find our way home. While that is MOSTLY true, it is not ALWAYS true, and on that Most Terrible of Days it was NOT true. Or maybe my Unique Blend just doesn't have the best hunting/searching/tracking skills. Whatever the case, I ran down every street in Limerick Beach, uphill and downhill, through alleys and tunnels and all along the beach. Soon it got dark. My eyes were wide open, my senses on full alert, my focus on one thing only - White House with Blue Trim, White House with Blue Trim … on Stutter Street or Strummer Street or something like that.

But - I cringe to be reminded - I never found a white house with blue trim and the rancid smell of three Dobermans next door.

By dawn my paw pads were worn and raw. I finally dropped from exhaustion at a Toys-R-Us parking lot and I slept under an abandoned car -

Oops - feeding time here at the shelter. Being as I can't multi-task, and need to concentrate whole-heartedly on the simple pleasure of EATING, I will have to finish telling my tale of the Most Terrible of Days another time.

CHAPTER 5

After returning the Dobermans to Mrs. Harper, Danielle realizes how late it is. She grabs her backpack and skateboard and rushes out to the sidewalk, where she sees her father across the street approaching home from the other direction.

"*Buenos días, Papa,*" she calls out, but coolly.

"*Hola! Cómo estás?*" he replies, hoping she'll wait for him and offer a hug.

None is forthcoming: she turns and goes inside the house. Nonetheless, it's a good sign that she's speaking Spanish to him again, as this is their special form of communication that no one else in the family can understand. She hasn't used it with him since the day he abandoned Beckett at the park.

(Boy, can I think of a few bad words in Spanish to say to him! But I'm not there. And dogs can't speak human words - yet!)

The three Dobermans are at the front window next door, drooling as they watch Danielle disappear into her house, which is a two-story white house with pale blue trim. A dense bougainvillea with crimson blooms covers the brick chimney.

Once inside the screened front porch, Danielle drops the skateboard and her backpack on the floor, and sinks into the hammock that's strung across a corner. She reaches for the book that's tucked inside the hammock and opens it at the bookmarked page. Down below on the wood-slat floor, Flopsie nibbles at a slice of apple. The rabbit must have been out of her cage all day - there are rabbit pellets scattered everywhere. Danielle gets back up, gathers the pellets with a tissue that she dumps into the waste basket, and flops back into the hammock to read her book.

Without missing a word, she reaches for Flopsie and hauls her - apple chunk and all - onto her chest.

The screen door squeaks closed behind Sam as he walks over to kiss the top of her head on his way into the house. Sam's the sports coach and gym teacher at the local high school and he's worn out after a long day.

Before he's even set his sports bag down, Simon and his friend Jerry, who has a head of thick black hair and bright blue eyes, gallop toward him and surround him. Simon pulls his father's arm.

"Let's go, Dad. C'mon!"

"What, no 'Hello'?"

"Hello. Let's go."

Jerry pipes in, "Howdy, Coach."

The boys follow Sam who walks through the house whistling loudly at Pickle, who whistles back. Simon's impatient.

"Dad, you told me to wait. I waited. Come on, you promised to run with us!"

Sam passes through the kitchen into the study. He drops his sports bag on top of the desk that's piled with papers, magazines and unopened mail. He thumbs through a sports magazine with one hand and, with the other hand, throws all the mail into a trash basket without looking at a single piece. The boys are right behind him. Finally he looks up from the magazine.

"Look, Simon, I didn't mean for you and Jerry to wait. I meant, just in case I felt like running. As it happens … I don't feel like it."

Danielle overhears from the porch and rolls her eyes.

Simon's face turns stormy. "Dad, you promised!"

Now it's Sam who's irritated. Sarcastically, he says, "If you're so hot to run, you two run. You don't need me."

Simon's embarrassed. Jerry backs away, tugging at Simon's sleeve.

"Come on, Si."

"You did this last week, Dad. All you ever want to do is put your feet up and drink things that stink."

Simon lets the door slam behind him.

Sam climbs the stairway and disappears into the bedroom, emerging moments later in shorts and a faded sweatshirt. He whistles as he walks back down the stairway and into the kitchen to the silver refrigerator from which he takes a can of beer and pops the top.

Pickle waits for him to whistle again. Sam doesn't, but returns to the porch, lowering himself into the comfy old white rattan couch. He takes a few long sips and lets out a sigh of relief. From the porch windows the setting sun pours in.

"Hey, Dad," Danielle asks from behind her book, "What do you call someone who can sit on a Lifesaver and tell you what color it is?"

"What?"

"A smart ass."

He laughs, sips.

"Here's one," Sam says lowering the beer can. "If a lemon fell into the ocean and was drowning what would you do?"

"Squeeze it?"

"No. You would Give … The … Lemon … Aid."

Danielle fakes a laugh, startling Flopsie, who has finished eating the apple and begun gnawing on the mesh of the hammock. Flopsie looks up to see what's going on, twitching her nose more than usual.

(I'm sure Danielle did appreciate her father's corny joke, but didn't want him to have the satisfaction of really laughing at it. After all, if it hadn't been for him, and that Most Terrible of Days, I would be in the hammock alongside her, getting my tummy rubbed, instead of being here on a cement floor at the shelter. No hammocks! No tummy rubs! Prison!)

A little while later, as Sam pops the top on his second beer, Danielle puts down her book and goes into the kitchen. She returns with a glass of iced tea from a pitcher in the refrigerator.

"Here, Dad. Try this instead."

To please her he takes a sip. Iced tea in one hand, beer can in the other, he sips one, then the other, until Danielle's face is hidden once again behind her book. Then he puts the iced tea glass down on the windowsill and goes back to the beer.

The sun sinks quickly at this time of year. As soon as it's gone, it becomes dark and the lights on the tiers of houses that go all the way to the ocean begin to twinkle. No one has turned on the light in the kitchen, though, and Pickle waits in his cage in the dark for someone to do so. He doesn't like being alone in the dark, especially since in days gone by, it was Beckett who would sometimes keep him company.

(Of course, if truth be told, I was really there just waiting for my dinner! But that bird didn't need to know that it was FOOD and not his - how shall I say - "debonair" personality that was keeping me there.)

CHAPTER 6

Glowing headlights from a small black car illuminate the dark driveway of the Godot house. As the car pulls in, it almost collides with a bicycle leaning against the dumpster by the garage. Shadows ripple against the side of the house, then the headlights are turned off. A tall woman with short red hair gets out and moves the bike aside. When she does, she sees a pair of green garden gloves lying on the dumpster lid.

She's Minnie, wife of Sam and mother of Danielle and Simon.

(She used to call me Becky, short for Beckett. When she and I were alone in the kitchen she'd always give me generous scraps of beef from the stew she was preparing or a piece of cookie when she was baking a fresh batch. I sure liked Minnie!)

The door squeaks behind her when she steps onto the porch carrying an armload of brown grocery bags. Sam stands up and takes the bags, carrying them into the kitchen, bashing his elbow against the doorframe on his way in.

Noticing Danielle on the hammock, Minnie turns back and comments, "Don't read in the dark, Baby," then switches on the overhead light.

Danielle grits her teeth - she hates it when her parents call her "baby." "I'm eleven, not four!" she mumbles. "Almost twelve!"

Minnie straightens her back and strides into the kitchen, calling sharply, "Simon!"

"I'm upstairs, Mom."

"How many times do I have to tell you not to lean your bike against the dumpster?" she yells with a shrill voice. "I almost hit it, you idiot!"

"Sorry, Mom, I'm only human!" Simon shouts back.

This irritates Minnie even more. "Don't be a smart aleck!" she yells.

Danielle jumps up and pokes her nose inside to see what's going on. Flopsie doesn't like it and hides her head between her paws.

Getting no reply, Minnie shouts even louder, "DO YOU HEAR ME?"

Simon appears on the landing of the stairway. He doesn't say anything, just stares nervously down at her.

Minnie's face is getting red. "I SAID, 'DO YOU HEAR ME?'"

Sam rushes over and reaches for her, "Whoa, whoa, Minnie. Calm down, eh?"

He wraps his arm over his wife's shoulder. "Get a grip, he's just a kid."

Minnie's shakes her head as if she's just woken up and Danielle's heart is pounding. Minnie never used to raise her voice. But lately …she's turning into a witch.

"Except that her skin isn't green, and she has no cool flying monkeys to swoop down at us," Danielle mumbles as she returns to the hammock and her book.

CHAPTER 7

Sam and Minnie stand at the kitchen counter beside the refrigerator. Minnie's eyes are swollen from crying. The bright overhead light is on, and Pickle moves from the upper to lower perch in his cage, always upset when someone is shedding tears.

Not wanting to miss anything, Danielle hovers in the doorway, chewing on the nail of her thumb.

Through her tears Minnie asks Sam, "What's wrong with me?"

(If I were there, lying under the kitchen table as usual, I'd tell her this: "YOU?!? It's that lame husband of yours who is making all of you nutty. He loses me in the park, he sits drinking beer all afternoon, and he plays moronic music at all hours of the night." But then I would add: "And you, Minnie, are becoming a real Drama Queen. You never used to be this way.")

Sam pulls a square of paper towel from a roll and hands it to Minnie, who blows her nose. She turns the faucet on, and splashes some water on her face. Pickle whistles loudly.

Danielle asks, "What did a piece of ice say, Mommy?"

"I don't know. What?" Minnie responds, drying her face with a dishtowel.

"It said, 'Keep cool'."

Her mother tries to force a smile, but one won't come.

Danielle shrugs her shoulders and struts off.

Minnie takes a deep breath and starts emptying the grocery bags, removing a cake box tied with string. Opening the counter drawer, she rummages through it looking for a knife with which to cut the string, then stops, staring down into the drawer.

"Sam! Someone's taping up the knives again!" She pulls out a large butcher knife that's been taped around with ugly, silver tape.

"Why would anyone do such a stupid, scary thing?"

"I don't know. It's creepy, Sam."

(I'd be the first to agree. It IS creepy. But I didn't do it. I'm too far away for that. And besides, dog paws can't unroll and wrap tape. Yet!)

Sam takes two cans of beer from the refrigerator.

"A beer, hon? It might settle you down."

Minnie pulls off the tape and lays the knife beside the cake box.

"Why not?"

He hugs her close.

Arm-in-arm, they walk towards the porch, each with a beer in hand. Once again Pickle is alone in the kitchen with only the plop of the leaking faucet for company. But at least the light's been left on.

(I don't know if that was just a hissy fit, or more family melodrama, but, man! At this particular moment I'm glad I'm not there!)

CHAPTER 8

Reaching the porch before her parents, Danielle picks up the beer can her dad had left earlier. She takes a little sip, opens the door to the front garden, pours the remaining fluid onto the bougainvillea and places the empty can back where it had been.

Arriving with cans of beer in hand, Minnie and Sam sit on the rattan sofa, shoulders touching. Minnie notices the second beer can on the side table.

"Ah, I see you started without me."

Stretched out on the hammock, Danielle realizes they're both drinking now and tightens her grip on the book.

Minnie reaches over and squeezes her daughter's bony foot. She asks in a honey-coated voice, "What are you reading, Dani-doo?"

Danielle pulls her foot away. She doesn't like it when they call her Dani-doo anymore. Dani-doo sounds like a name for a leprechaun or a cartoon mouse.

"'Guardians of Ga'Hoole'," she mumbles without looking up.

Sam stretches out and grabs the beer can he'd left earlier. He shakes it, surprised to find it empty since he doesn't remember finishing it.

"Did you get to your physical this afternoon?" Minnie asks him.

"Yup," he answers.

"Well?"

"Everything's fine. The doctor suggested some tests."

Danielle looks up. "If everything's so fine, Daddy, then why do they want you to have tests?"

"You know how doctors are."

"No, how are they?" she wonders sarcastically.

"Oh, they just like to give tests."

Sam takes a long drink, emptying the second can. "Another beer?" he asks his wife, standing up.

"I'll take a sip from yours. I've got to cook soon."

"I'll have one," Danielle responds. "Make mine a grande, please."

"Very funny," Sam snaps and walks out.

"Didn't you just read 'Guardians of Ga'Hoole', all fifteen in the series?" Minnie asks, when they are alone.

"Yeah. I'm reading all the books again. I'm on number twelve, 'The Golden Tree'." Danielle scornfully comments, "You know, you only make it worse by joining him."

"What do you mean?"

Danielle climbs out of the hammock.

"You know what I mean ... gulp, gulp, gulp." Then adds, "I've got homework!" as she rushes out of the room.

She leaps up the stairs two steps at a time and lets her bedroom door bang behind her. It feels good to slam something, but not quite good enough, so she throws the book at her bed, which makes her feel a little better.

She stares at one of the many photos of her lost dog tacked onto the wall. "God, I miss you, Beckett," she says to the photo, "SO much! Don't give up on me. I'll find you, I won't give up!"

(Wow, I heard that! I really heard that! See, I told you we dogs have secret bonds with our owners. Now let me try: 'Come, Danielle, come! I'm at some rusty-roofed dog shelter near a burger joint. I know, 'cuz I can smell French fries twenty-four seven. Come get me, PLEASE!')

CHAPTER 9

Another beer in hand, Sam changes his mind about sitting back down and picks up Flopsie, who has chewed another piece of the hammock. He leaves with her and climbs the stairs to the second floor, leaving Minnie by herself on the porch.

He walks into Simon's room and puts Flopsie inside her cage, where Simon has piled a meal of iceberg lettuce and parsley. Simon sits on the lower bunk bed looking at something. Next to the cage leans a guitar that Simon begged for but seldom practices. On his wall are two posters of Professor Dumbledore from the Harry Potter films, and a blown-up photo of Simon and Sam at one of Simon's soccer matches the previous year.

"Hey, why didn't you sign up for soccer again this year, Si?" Sam asks while gazing at the photo.

"I dunno. Didn't feel like it."

"Doesn't matter, Si. I just asked," Sam softly comments.

Spread out on the bed in front of Simon is an almost-complete collection of Harry Potter cards that he keeps in a small wooden box. When he's grumpy (which is more and more often these days), he likes to take them out and classify them in different groups: kids versus adults, good people versus bad people, wizards versus muggles. He's holding up one of Snape and reading the back and doesn't acknowledge his dad. Sam tries again.

"Hey. I've got a great idea, Dude."

Simon still doesn't look up. "I'm checking out my cards, Dad."

When Sam lurches to sit on the edge of the bed, beer sloshes out of the can onto some of the cards.

Simon snaps. "Dad! HEY!"

"Sorry, Si! Come on, let's go take a run."

Simon points at the window. "It's dark, Dad. Can't you see?"

He wipes beer off the cards with his bed sheet, then sniffs to see if they stink of beer. Just slightly.

"Don't be a fuddy-duddy. It's a great time for a run. A moonlit jog."

Simon's not very keen, but gets to his feet anyway, leaving the cards spread out to dry.

Back downstairs, where Danielle has brought her homework to do, she watches her father and brother pass by in running gear.

"Care to join us, Dani?" Sam calls as they head out the doorway. "I need you kids for good luck. First game's on Friday and my quarterback sucks."

She shakes her head, but watches them wistfully.

"Hey, wait!" she yells, changing her mind and pushing her homework aside.

Already wearing sneakers, she hurries after them. Sam pats her back as she catches up and the three jog side by side.

"A run on the beach, a moon swim with my two kids. Is this the life, or what?"

(It'd be an even better life, Mr. Sam, if you had your dog at your side too! Remember D-O-G, dog? Beckett? Lost dog? Abandoned dog?)

They head down the hill toward the glinting lights of their town, then cut over to the beach.

Soon they are running along the hard wet sand beside the foamy surf. At the sight of the immense sea, Danielle's resentment fades away. Soon she starts blabbing. She tells her father about a dream she has had two times recently.

"In the dream someone keeps asking me for string, but I don't have any. In the jar where I once kept string there's only honey that has crystallized, and it's hard as a rock. At the end of the dream, I pass a window where I can see my own reflection. And, guess what, Dad? I'm headless. I'm like carrying my own head under my arm!"

"That's gross!" Simon mutters.

Running side by side at a lazy clip, Sam listens. That his daughter is confiding in him like she used to gives him a warm glow inside, even if her dreams are a bit disturbing.

They run until the warm lights of Limerick Beach town are far behind.

CHAPTER 10

Later that night, dinner eaten, tooth-brushing done, Simon and Danielle, along with Flopsie and Pickle, are (in theory) fast asleep.

But not so.

Danielle has tiptoed down the stairs into the kitchen. Dirty dishes are piled up in the sink. The faucet drips onto a pan, making a pinging sound. A pot that contains leftover pasta stands on the counter alongside bits of limp salad. The remainder of the carrot cake they had for dessert has been returned to the cake box.

Pickle lets out a little chirp; he, too, is wide awake. Danielle changes his water and clips a sheaf of millet to the cage as a treat. She opens the refrigerator and takes a sip from a carton of apple juice. Spotting two cans of beer, she takes them out and hides them in the cabinet below the sink, far back behind the laundry detergent. Pickle chirps again when she reaches up and lowers his cage from its hook. It's pretty big but she hugs it to her chest.

Cage in arms, she tiptoes down the hall passing the living room door. It is dark inside, but from the shadows she can see that her parents are there. They're sitting side by side on the floor watching the fire in the fireplace, sipping red wine in glasses that reflect the light from the fire. Music from some old 80's band is playing as Minnie rubs the back of

Sam's neck. Danielle hears her say: "You've got a real knot there, Hon."

Clumsily, Sam stands up when the song ends, tripping over his running shoes. He walks over to the old CD player, and begins the same song again. Sliding back down beside Minnie, he nearly knocks over his wine glass, then burps.

Minnie stands up. "Let's go to sleep, Sam."

Danielle quickly climbs the stairway lugging Pickle. It's Simon's night to have Flopsie, so she's glad to have Pickle for company.

(In my opinion a parakeet is a sorry substitute for a cuddly dog. I'd be there in a minute if I knew the way home. But I don't, so Danielle has to settle for a stiff green bird to keep her company in the dark of night instead of furry, soft, warm moi.)

Back in her room, Danielle puts the cage on her desk, opening its door so that Pickle can get out during the night to roost on her head while she sleeps, if he wants. Danielle's eyes and ears are wide open as she settles into bed. She's waiting to hear the sound of her parents climbing the stairs to go to bed, so she knows everything is OK.

Back in the living room, Minnie is waiting for Sam to get up.

"I just want to hear the end of this CD."

"You've heard it four times already, Sam."

"Shh. This is thee best part."

Minnie shakes her head and walks out of the room.

Danielle hears the sound of her mother coming up the stairs, and the music still going on, and rolls over.

Alone now, Sam stares into bright red flames while sipping more wine.

(Oh gosh, my favorite thing: sitting by the fire! If I were there, I'd be sitting with him. Instead I'm freezing my butt off in an unheated shelter.)

Slowly the fire burns down. One of Sam's Nike shoes that he accidentally kicked into the hearth starts to melt but Sam hasn't noticed, even though it stinks of burnt rubber. He's enthralled by a photo album he's taken down from a shelf that has pictures of Sam and Minnie in Greece when they were much younger. One photo is the two of them in front of the marble Parthenon, another on a white ship. They are smiling.

He keeps playing the same song over and over.

And upstairs nobody sleeps very well. Not even Pickle.

CHAPTER 11

On their way to their various schools, Sam and Simon walk side by side along Limerick Beach Boulevard, and Danielle rides ahead, practicing laser flips on her skateboard. There's fog in the air, and a late September breeze rustles a few scraggly leaves down at their feet (and wheels). They are engaged in conversation, and closer than they've been in weeks.

"… But if Pickle really were a Buddhist he wouldn't eat insects, would he?" Simon asks.

"No, I guess not. He'd be a vegetarian, I suppose, eating tofu flies or soya ants or something."

"Yuck."

Simon takes the moment to complain that his sister was supposed to clean Flopsie's cage and Pickle's cage all week but, so far, she hasn't cleaned either. "I did them both last week. And really did them," Simon concludes.

Danielle skates toward them, then does an abrupt flip turn-around and is rolling alongside. "Hey, where do cars get the most flat tires?"

Simon asks, "Where?"

"Where there is a FORK in the road."

Sam rolls his eyes. Simon does, too.

Just ahead of them a man in his mid-twenties, bearded, sleeves rolled up, a tattoo of a jet plane decorating his forearm, gets off his motorcycle. The elaborate tattoo attracts Danielle's attention and she jumps off her skateboard.

Noticing Sam, the man calls out, "Hey, kalimera, Mr. Godot," wishing him a good morning in Greek.

Startled, Sam looks curiously at him.

"Hey, you coming in today?" the young man asks Sam.

Sam shows no recognition, says, "You must be mistaken. I don't know you."

The man is bewildered as Sam speeds up his pace, pulling both kids with him.

"Who's he?" Danielle asks.

"I never saw that guy before in my life," Sam replies.

The whole encounter seems strange to Danielle, but she's fascinated by the tattoos and turns around to take another look.

CHAPTER 12

At the middle school where she enrolled just weeks before, Danielle goes to her seventh grade class and takes her seat beside Nicky, who has on one of his many Superman T-shirts. He bops her on the head with a catalogue he has rolled up in his hand. It's weird to be out of grade school, so she's really glad she and Nicky are still together in the new school. She hands him half her power bar, down low so nobody sees.

He opens the catalogue to point out the new skateboard he's hoping to get for his birthday next month. It is long and sleek and the wheels are dayglow green.

"Wow, cool," she comments enthusiastically. "But what if it goes so fast that I can't keep up with you?"

"Then I guess I'll have to wait up for you, like you always do for me," he laughs.

The teacher walks in and all the kids get quiet.

Nearby, after recess at the local grade school, Simon sits at his desk in his fourth grade class. Marta, who sits next to him and who, along with Simon, is the best in math, sees him fiddling with some small figurines in his lap. Recognizing them she asks, "You prefer Gimli or Legolas?"

"Legolas. He's so cool with his bow and arrows."

"Yeah, me, too," Marta smiles at him, then opens her notebook wide to reveal a large photo of Legolas the elf, taped on the inside cover.

Simon grins. "Yeah, if Aragorn wasn't the king, I'd vote for Legolas. Or my dad …," then pauses and adds, "Well, I'm not so sure about my dad these days."

Meanwhile, feeling a little queasy, Sam strolls across the high school playing field. He passes a grass corridor where dozens of bikes are parked. There's a poster on the wall beyond the bike-racks:

FIRST GAME OF THE SEASON,
FRIDAY NIGHT.
GET OUT AND CHEER OUR TEAM!

Sam enters the boys' locker room, opens his locker, and changes into a warm-up suit, lowering the string that holds his whistle onto his neck.

Leaving the locker room, he walks down the hall to his office. After shutting the door, he takes a bottle of Maalox out of the desk drawer and pours a spoonful, making a sour face as he swallows. It's a chalky white liquid medicine for soothing the stomach and he burps. He looks at his watch and realizes he'd better hurry to the gym, where his freshman boys are waiting.

Once there, he makes sure all the boys are wearing the proper gym shorts and Limerick Beach High T-shirts, and then leads them through a drill of warm-up exercises. When the boys begin to moan, Sam loudly proclaims: "No pain, no gain. C'mon, keep it up!" though he is a bit out of breath himself.

Out of the corner of his eye, Sam observes one of the biggest boys tripping a smaller boy, and blows his whistle. He helps the smaller boy up and turns to the others.

"Hey, listen gentlemen, and listen well! Sports are all about cooperation. And respect. So there will be no bullying, AT ALL. Understood?"

Everyone nods and someone mumbles, "Yeah."

Sam pats the smaller boy's shoulder and then, turns and pats the taller one's shoulder, too.

"I mean it. Zero tolerance. Now let's work up a little sweat."

He blows the whistle.

(Ok, this is the time of day I REALLY miss not being at the Godot home! Late morning was the best time, other than nightly cuddles with Danielle. By now all the humans were at school or at their jobs, and I'd be alone in the house with the pooper and the whistler. I'd get to snooze in the silence of the empty house, jump up and sleep on any couch, any bed, knowing that at day's end my family would be returning home, and

then one or another, usually Danielle, would take me to the dog park and throw balls or Frisbees or sticks for some fun. But that won't be happening again anytime soon! And she'll never know that the very last time we played that game in a park I chipped one of my teeth on a hard stick and lost my cute grin. Oh, gosh! I hope she can still recognize me when she finds me!)

After Sam's gym class ends, he wraps a towel around his sweaty neck and pops back into his office for another spoonful of Maalox. Rex Cunningham, a history teacher and friend, follows him into the office asking, "Can I take you to lunch?"

"Sure, but why should you TAKE me?"

"To soothe your ruffled feathers."

"Are they ruffled?"

"You're hopeless, Sam. Duke's just gotten the chairmanship you should have gotten and you behave like -"

Seeing Sam's surprise, he asks, "Didn't you know?"

Sam shakes his head.

Embarrassed, Rex adds, "I assumed you knew. Everyone knows."

"Duke Kelly got it! Minnie was counting on ME getting it," Sam laments.

Just then, Dr. Jefferson, the school principal, a distinguished older African-American man with a mustache, passes in the hall. Sam calls out, "Dr. Jefferson, can I see you a sec?"

Dr. Jefferson gives Sam a big grin and stops at the doorway.

"Hope you gave them a good workout, Sam."

"I did. But, uh, tell me ... why did Duke get the chairmanship?" Sam asks sheepishly. "That promotion should have been mine."

"You're right, Sam. It should have been."

"Then why?"

"That's what I'd like to know. What's going on with you, Sam? Where's your old spark, your enthusiasm? You are absent much too much ..." Dr. Jefferson's voice softens, "Are there problems at home? Something bothering you?"

"Why is everyone asking me that?" Sam mutters.

CHAPTER 13

School's finished for the day, and Danielle skates home as fast as she can. She tries to do a Shove-It move but falls off, jamming her finger against the asphalt. She's been thinking all day about a new idea and wants to get home to try it out. Skateboard under her arm, she drops her backpack inside the porch, and heads next door holding her nose as she walks through Mrs. Harper's poop-filled, overgrown back yard.

The kitchen door is wide open, so she sticks her head in and calls out, "Hello?"

No Mrs. Harper. Instead all three dogs dash in and jump all over her. Cautiously, Danielle tip-toes into the living room and sees Mrs. Harper fast asleep on the couch.

With a pen and scrap of paper from the desktop, she writes a note that she leaves on the coffee table beside the couch. Grabbing the dogs' leashes, she goes back outside, while the three dogs excitedly follow behind.

Skateboard under her arm, she attaches each dog to its leash and they make their way through the garden. On the street Danielle is ready to try out her experiment, first calming the dogs as much as possible. Gingerly, she climbs onto her skateboard and jiggles the leashes. The dogs begin to walk, pulling her along atop her skateboard as if they were sled dogs and she were an Inuit in the Arctic. She shakes the leashes.

"C'mon, Dobies! GO!"

They break into a trot, pulling her briskly down the street.

(Dopey Dobermans — you can make them do ANYthing! Me, I'm more selective in my pursuits. Chasing a ball on the beach or riding in the car with my head hanging out the window — now, THERE'S an adventure! But there the dopes go, heading downhill, taking Danielle on a breathtaking ride as if they were ponies.

I have to admit that she hasn't looked this happy in a long time. Probably since she and Nicky and I discovered a long tunnel under a canal nearby and their squeals — and my yapping — echoed around and around. Now THAT was a grand day! A pox on Dobermans!)

CHAPTER 13 ½

It's me again, Beckett. I have been away from the Godot family so long that I wake up some days wondering if my life with them was all a dream. I'm bored, too. And the volunteer today is not dog-friendly. (He prefers CATS! Imagine! What a goon.) So it's a good time to finish telling the tale of that Most Terrible of Days. Where did I leave off?

Oh, yeah. After Sam abandoned me, I ran all over town looking for their house or their smell (even the stench of the three Dobermans next door would have guided me) and finally dropped from exhaustion at a Toys-R-Us parking lot, thinking I'd sleep under an abandoned car. Well, "sleep" is the wrong word. Let's say I lay there for a few hours and thought about the Godots' faces, but mostly Dani's. I thought about her soft bed and me NOT being there alongside her, but on gritty concrete instead, and about how worried she would be. If dogs could shed tears, I would have that night. But we can't so I won't lie and say I did. I may have whimpered a little, though.

The sunlight came too early for my taste, and a few cars started arriving in the parking lot, passing the abandoned car I was sleeping/not sleeping under. The store opened an hour later, and many more arrived, one stopping nearby with a family inside. As they clambered out, the youngest boy in the family spotted me and crouched down to check me out. He smiled and made that weird lip-smacking sound you humans do to call us and tapped his hand down on the pavement to encourage me over.

I was a bit afraid – I've been kicked by enough mean people to be cautious with your species. But his face was sweet, so I took a chance and scooted along and put my head near his out-stretched hand. He patted my head and when I scooted over closer, he nuzzled my ears. Ah! The way to a dog's heart: an ear nuzzle!

"Hey, get away from there!" a grown-up female voice shouted at the boy.

"But, Mom, there's a dog. He looks lonely and scared," the kid said.

"A dog! Where? I wanna see!" more little-kid voices squealed and suddenly four other wide-eyed faces were peering under the car at me. Five kids! That's ten hands! That's a lot of cuddling! I scooted over even more and – ah! bliss! – had ten little hands patting my head and nuzzling my neck and scrunching my ears and picking at my teeth (okay, one of those kids was a little weird).

The female voice from above yelled and all the kids - and hands! - moved away. So, I followed them and came out from under the car.

"Ahh, poor little doggy," the lady said when she saw me (okay, I confess, I put on my best Desperate Dog Face).

"Mommy, can we take him home? Can we have him? Huh? Please!" the kids blabbered all at once, and they were so cute jumping up and down on the pavement I didn't even mind them calling me "him."

So guess what that sweet family did? They changed all their plans and did NOT go in the Toys-R-Us, but instead carried me into their car, and the three kids in the back seat smothered me with kisses and pats.

"A Home! A Home! I'm Getting a New Home!" I sang to myself as we drove along, heading, so I thought, to their house.

Even that weird little kid picking at my teeth while the others petted me didn't deter from my immense joy.

Though Danielle's face did cross my mind in that car ride, and I felt a little guilty about abandoning my search for her, I was totally taken in by my new family.

So did that sweet family take me home and give me The Perfect Dog Life of ten little hands and four adult hands cuddling me day and night? Did I get my own doggy bed in the corner and two big meals a day and a huge yard to play in with all those little hyper-kiddies?

"Main Street Animal Shelter," the sign said as we pulled off the road into a small parking lot. Out the kids went. Out I followed. Then - WHAM! BAM! - I was forced into a small cage, alone and abandoned again! Second time in less than twenty-four hours! A dog could get a real complex from such things.

That was three weeks ago. 20 days and 14 hours, to be exact. I scratch slashes on the wall with a claw to keep track.

And I wait. And I wait.

DANIELLE, WHERE ARE YOU???

CHAPTER 14

It's Saturday and Danielle and Sam have driven to the local mega-market. He's pushing the shopping cart up an aisle, Danielle trailing behind with a checkered baby snuggly attached to her shoulders. Wrapped in it, Flopsie is a not-too-happy-rabbit who really doesn't like being taken on adventures. But, these days, Danielle likes having her around due to missing her dog so much.

Danielle follows behind Sam who is gloomy because his team lost yesterday's game. They didn't just lose, they were crushed. Demolished. Creamed. As they stroll, they pass a rack filled with self-help books. Sam stops, picks up a book titled, "Staying Young: Staying in Charge." He drops it into the cart.

Danielle grabs another, hands it to him, "Improving Your Memory: A Dozen Tricks." He slips this one into the cart, too.

(I wish there was one called "Finding Your Lost Dog before It's Too Late" - I'd put THAT one in the cart myself!)

Although she's not a lightweight anymore, Sam scoops Danielle up and throws her over his shoulder. Upside down, he actually gets her to giggle. This is what he used to always do with her when she was small. Now because she's much taller, she hangs past his knees, her head almost hitting the ground.

Flopsie slips out from the snuggly unnoticed and hops onto the floor. Sam, the cart, and upside-down Danielle move on. Flopsie's long ears perk up. She stops and looks around, nervously pooping some pellets.

After a few aisles, Danielle seems to be getting heavier so Sam turns her right-side-up and stands her back on her feet. They continue up and down the aisles while Sam picks things off the shelves and tosses them into the cart for a barbecue - salsa and chips, a six-pack of beer, a second six-pack, chicken parts, hot dogs, rolls, cans of dog food, bird seed, veggies for the rabbit, corn on the cob, and other picnic things like paper plates and cups, mustard.

As they approach the check-out counter, Danielle sees the cans of dog food in the cart, and a look of misery crosses her face. As she removes them, they move up to the register.

Suddenly she shouts. "Oh, my God! FLOPSIE!!!!"

She runs back through the store, looking down every aisle, until she sees Flopsie, who has found a basket of Spanish onions and has begun gnawing at one. Danielle scoops up the rabbit, holds her close, then slides her back into the snuggly. As an afterthought, she grabs a small, yellow onion and puts it into the snuggly to comfort the confused rabbit.

("Confused"? Flopsie is not confused. She is dippy, I tell ya, DIPPY. That's a rabbit for you. Not the greatest of pets. I mean, can a rabbit chase sticks? Raise a paw to shake? Roll over and play dead? Have you ever heard of a rabbit howling at the moon? Has any rabbit anywhere anytime hopped over to their master with the morning newspaper in its mouth??

Rabbits! Phooey!

And don't even get me started on CATS!)

CHAPTER 15

With the overflowing bags in the back seat of Sam's old blue Saab, he pulls out of the parking lot. While they drive through town, he complains about his inept quarterback. It's a bit boring, but Danielle listens. When he pauses, she pokes him.

"Hey, Dad. Do zombies like being dead?"

"I don't know. Do they?"

"Of corpse they do."

"Bueno, bueno!"

For a little while, it's like old times. Sam even detours to get Danielle her favorite ice cream cone - mint chip. His is usually Cherry Garcia, but since he's worrying about his paunch, he resists.

"So how are things with Nick?" he asks when they get back in the car.

"The same." she replies, licking a green drip of ice cream running down the cone.

"Really? He used to come over all the time. The tree-house hardly gets used anymore. Maybe you kids are getting too old for it?"

"No," she reassures him, which is not quite true.

They drive past a derelict building with broken windows and a dead lawn. It reminds her that he's been promising to repair the plank on the tree-house floor that split last spring but has continually put it off. Not wanting to rub his nose in it, she has stopped mentioning it.

"I never see your friend around the house, anymore. You ashamed of us, or something?" he asks, joking, but not joking.

"You're nuts!" Danielle feebly replies.

(Though really, she sort of means "yes" since Sam was tipsy, singing loudly and walking around wearing only boxer

shorts last time Nick visited. I know! I was there, hiding under the bed whimpering.)

Sam turns into the long driveway of the Hammond home. The Hammonds - Jean and Jeffrey - are family friends, and also the parents of Simon's best friend, Jerry. They live in an affluent neighborhood on the edge of Limerick Beach in a ranch-style house that has a swimming pool. They've invited the Godot family over for one last barbecue/swim before autumn really sets in.

Sam parks the car under the shade of a eucalyptus tree, and he and Danielle carry the shopping bags into the kitchen where everybody's busy getting things ready. Danielle takes Flopsie out of the snuggly and gives her a shake. The onion falls to the ground and rolls underneath the refrigerator. Flopsie watches it disappear as Danielle nuzzles her between her fuzzy ears while walking out alone across the patio where the pool, barbecue and lounges are.

She sets Flopsie on a chaise and blows up a rubber raft and drops it into the pool, then strips off her shorts and hoodie. Underneath she's wearing the bathing suit that the Hammonds gave her on her last birthday - blue and green checks - which she doesn't really like, but has put on because her mother begged her to.

She grabs the snuggly and Flopsie, and holding the book high in the air to keep it dry, climbs onto the float. Pushing off from the edge of the pool with her foot, she glides to the middle of the pool and opens her book.

Flopsie likes the sensation of floating. Also, she's tired after the car ride and closes her eyes though her nose keeps twitching.

Danielle is glad to get back into the story she's reading.

Soon Sam has put on his bathing suit and comes out back. Jean Hammond follows. She's a plumpish woman with bleached blonde hair (now hidden under a wide-brim hat), wearing a bright red one-piece swimsuit speckled with black dots that makes Danielle giggle, since it reminds her of a big ladybug.

Sam stretches out on a chaise lounge next to Jean. who's sipping a Bloody Mary. Jean's husband, Jeffrey, a doctor, usually called Jeff by his friends, is tall and pleasant, with the same thick black hair as his son Jerry. Entering the pool area, he hands Sam a Bloody Mary.

(A Bloody Mary, let me tall ya, tastes like tomato juice and spices and cleaning fluid. I know this since I tasted some once when a plastic glass was kicked over at a summer pool party - ugh.)

Jeff bustles busily around the barbecue. His plastic apron has a drawing of a cartoon mouse wearing a chef's hat on it. He loves to wear the same apron at all the barbecues, and it always makes Danielle smirk.

(Danielle finds the cartoon as lame as I would have. I mean, a cartoon dog, okay. Sure. Why not? Could be Snoopy

or Scooby-Doo. But a mouse on a cooking apron? Mice have no class. Might as well have a cartoon flea on it.)

When Jeff pours lighter fluid on the coals and tosses in a lit match, there is an explosive Swoosh!, and Flopsie trembles.

Carrying a tray from the kitchen, Minnie sets it over on the folding table beside the big fancy outdoor barbecue. She lines up hot dogs and chicken parts with tongs; in a separate corner, tofu dogs for Jean.

"Once again we do all the work while our beloveds rest on their broadening derrieres," she comments to Jeff. "And, of course, my not-so-little daughter hasn't lifted a finger, either."

Danielle uses one hand to paddle towards the far edge of the pool.

Sam drains his glass. He stands up, takes off and folds his Hawaiian shirt, stretches, and asks no one and everyone, "Swim?"

Jean responds, "No, thanks. I just had my hair done."

He turns to Minnie. "Swim?"

"In a minute, I'm helping to cook, Dear."

He dives into the pool, coming up behind Danielle and wrapping his arms around her shoulders. Drops of water splash her book.

"Hey, Dad, c'mon!" she warns sternly, "You're wetting my book. And Flopsie doesn't like water. Also, she's sleeping. Was!"

Sam backs off. He starts swimming very fast, doing the Australian crawl up and down the length of the pool. When he climbs out, he touches his toes a couple of times, does a few push-ups and finally attempts a head stand (although the extra roll of fat around his middle sags a bit), and nearly crashes over.

He's breathless by the time he flops back down onto the chaise.

"I used to be able to do hundreds of these. Now … I'm just like my lazy football team."

Danielle looks up from her book.

"Oh, Dad, you still could if you REALLY wanted to."

He wipes himself with his towel.

"I take it your team lost," Jean comments.

Sam sighs.

"Tryin' to be nice, Jean? The whole town knows we didn't just lose …" He looks crestfallen, "We … got slaughtered!"

He refills his glass from a pitcher that's on the table. As he's about to collapse back down on the chaise, Minnie slips into the pool.

"Sam, time for the swim you promised me."

He turns to jump in and slips, bashing his knee on a planter before clumsily falling into the water.

Danielle paddles even further away until there's nowhere else to go.

CHAPTER 16

The sun disappears behind a wisp of cloud and the pool appears darker blue.

Wearing their Cub Scout uniforms, Simon and Jerry arrive home; Danielle can see them through the kitchen window. They are returning after a cookie bake-off and sale, and Simon carries a platter covered with foil that contains samples of their cookies. They slide open the glass doors bringing them to the pool area. Jerry is thin, and his puff of jet black hair make him seem taller than Simon.

Seeing the boys, Jeff jumps up from his recliner.

"Hey, how'd it go?"

"Great, Dad. We made snickerdoodles and didn't burn one!" Jerry replies.

"These are leftovers," Simon says as he lays the platter on the table.

"Good one, guys. Let me throw some more dogs on the barbecue. How hungry are you?"

"Starved!" Jerry growls.

"Superstarved!" Simon yells louder.

Minnie pours glasses of lemonade for the boys, which they gulp down before rushing inside to put on their bathing suits.

Jerry's back first and cannonballs into the pool, splashing water in every direction.

"Boo! Only six point nine," Danielle laughs.

"What'da ya mean?" Jerry asks.

"In the Limerick Beach Olympics that jump only gets a six point nine."

"Oh, yeah. Watch this!"

Jerry climbs out to make another attempt and sees Simon arrive in a blue bathing suit that's a bit baggy.

"Hurry, Si. Olympic Champinchips!"

"Champ-EE-onships," Danielle corrects him.

"Just a sec," Simon replies, walking toward his mother gripping an envelope stuffed with money that's wrapped with a rubber band.

"How do you get a money order, Mom?" he asks Minnie.

"Why?" Minnie wonders, sitting at the pool's edge dangling her feet in the water.

"We're going to Big Elk Mountain for our Harvest Moon weekend and I'm the treasurer."

Jeff holds a paper plate filled with hot dogs, corn on the cob and potato salad. Seeing it, his son gets out of the pool and takes the plate.

"Thanks, Dad."

Jerry sits at the edge of the pool besides Minnie so he, too, can dangle his feet in the cool water. He wolfs down a hotdog. Jeff hands Simon the next plate when it's filled.

(This is where, had I been there, I would have been able to grab a hot dog or two off the grill for myself without anyone noticing. I can't even remember my last hot dog! I'm so desperate these days, I'd even steal one of Jean's tofu dogs!)

Simon walks over to his father's chaise and sits on the edge. He sets the plate down beside him on the chaise.

"I've got to send a money order to reserve a cabin for our troop."

"Any post office does money orders," Jeff explains.

"Give it here, Son," Sam reaches out his hand. "I've got to stop at the post office on Monday to mail some bills. I'll get the money order and send it for you."

Danielle looks up from her book and listens.

"It's got to get to Big Elk by Friday, Dad."

"No problem. Give me the address. Your food's getting cold."

"The address is already written on the envelope."

Simon hesitates, but then hands his father the envelope filled with cash. "Dad, this is serious. You can't forget!"

"I won't forget," Sam replies, defensively. "Don't you trust your old dad?"

"You forgot Beckett and she disappeared," Simon reminds him in a hostile tone of voice.

Protectively, Minnie chimes in, "Simon, it was an accident."

Danielle interjects caustically from where she floats in the pool, "Hey, Simon! Remember how last week Dad forgot that he gave us our allowances, and then gave them to us again!"

Everyone laughs at this.

"Ha, ha," Sam replies sarcastically as he stuffs the envelope into the pocket of his Hawaiian shirt.

Simon digs into his corn on the cob, as Jean circulates with the Bloody Mary pitcher, refilling the adults' glasses. When she gets to Jeff, he puts his hand over his glass, signaling No More.

Meanwhile, the barbecue begins smoking profusely; Jeff has neglected some chicken wings.

(Had I been there, I'd have been salivating beside the barbecue. I'd have noticed that the wings were getting scorched. And scarfed them down anyway.)

CHAPTER 17

The sun is behind the treetops. Simon and Jerry have gone to the new superhero movie in town, and Danielle has just gone inside to change. Plates are stacked with chicken bones, cobs minus corn and salad bits on the circular glass table beside the pool. There are also small plates containing watermelon rinds and crumbs of leftover chocolate cake and snickerdoodles.

Jeff chews on a burnt chicken wing while Sam and Jean, still glued to their adjoining chaises, empty the pitcher of Bloody Marys. Jean's giddy and Sam's feeding Flopsie bits of cilantro from the salad when Minnie emerges from the house dressed in street clothes. Her red hair is wet and freshly combed.

"We lost one of Sam's Nike's the other day and now both of Danielle's have vanished. Anybody see Dani's red sneakers?" she asks.

Spying them behind the stone planter filled with red geraniums, Jeff reaches over and grabs them.

"Feel like a film, Hon?" Minnie asks Sam as she takes the shoes from Jeff. "There's a good one in Belleville."

"I'm feeling lazy," he sighs, folding his fists behind his head.

Jeff dumps bones and plates into a black garbage bag.

Minnie tries again. "How about a walk on the pier? Check out the surfers?"

"In a little while …"

"But Sam, it's after five, maybe Jean and Jeff have -"

"Nu-shing of the sort." Jean cuts in, slurring her words.

"Let's just hang out. Have one for the road, Babe. C'mon," Sam sputters.

"How 'bout an Irish coffee?" Jean suggests.

That sounds good to Sam. "Why don't I meet you guys at the pier in half an hour?" he tells Minnie, who has lost the sparkle in her eyes.

Danielle wanders out through the sliding glass doors. She's dressed in jeans and a checked shirt but her feet are bare. "Mom, I can't find my -"

Minnie hands her the sneakers. "You and your dad and shoes!"

She puts them on and picks up Flopsie.

"Thanks for inviting us," Danielle says to the Hammonds.

"Hey, Dani, why don't you leave Flopsie with me?" Sam suggests.

A look of panic crosses Danielle's face. Without replying to her father's offer, she hangs the snuggly over her shoulders, placing Flopsie gently in it.

After Danielle, Minnie and Flopsie have gone, Jean again suggests, "Irish coffee, then? Steaming, creamy, Irish yummy coffee." And adds, "… with a witto-bitty splash of Jameson whiskey?"

Sam stands up. "Sure. I'll fix them."

He wraps a towel around his waist, as the pool is now completely in shadow and it's quickly cooling off. He almost slips while crossing the patio, and goes inside, closing the sliding glass door behind him.

He's gotta pee first, but can't remember where the bathroom is.

CHAPTER 18

The sun has sunk into the ocean with only melting red and golden ripples reflected in the water. Minnie has hung Flopsie and the snuggly over her shoulder because Danielle's atop her skateboard, rolling along just ahead on the pier. She stops to look down over the railing at the surfers, lying motionless on their surfboards, waiting for a good wave. Minnie catches up and stands beside her.

Danielle bends down and picks up her skateboard. She'd like to say something about her father, but decides against it. Instead she takes a Sharpie out of her pocket and draws an elephant on the bottom of her skateboard beside a decal.

"How can you tell if there's an elephant in the refrigerator?" she asks her mother, instead.

"How?" her mother wonders.

"The door won't shut."

"Cute."

"I'm collecting elephant jokes. Want to hear another one?"

"Sure."

"Why is an elephant large, gray and wrinkled?"

"Why?"

"Because if he were small, white and round he'd be an aspirin."

"I've got to digest that one," responds Minnie, tongue in cheek.

"Hey, that's good, Mom. Aspirin … digest … I get it."

Minnie gives her a thumbs up.

"Mom?"

"What?"

"What do people mean when they say, 'An elephant in the room?' I don't get it and it's not even funny."

"It's not a joke, honey, it's a saying." Minnie replies, "It's when there's something that should be obvious, like, say, someone's got a big pimple on the end of their nose, but no one mentions it. Or remember when your grannie had cancer and we never discussed it in front of her? See, it's like there's this huge elephant in the middle of the room and everyone's pretending there's nothing there and just squeeze past it. Get it?"

Danielle isn't sure.

Minnie turns serious and asks, "Dani, girl to girl … can I ask you something?"

"Sure," Danielle replies, even if she is a bit scared of what it might be about.

"Do you like my new haircut?"

Danielle nods.

"Do you think Daddy likes it?"

"How would I know?" she answers, glad the question wasn't about what she thought it was going to be about. But also a little disappointed that it wasn't.

Minnie pats at her hair that's rippling in the wind. Flopsie doesn't like wind and has tucked her head down into her neck.

"Speaking of elephants, I hope it doesn't make me look fat."

"You're not fat, Mom. It's stupid that you think so."

Danielle looks down again at the surfers. One has caught a surging wave and rides across the golden reflection of sunset on the water.

"Hmm," Danielle thinks to herself. "I wonder if surfing is just skateboarding on waves?""

CHAPTER 19

Back at the Hammond's poolside, now deep in shadow, Jean sings along as an Abba song blasts out of the speakers. Her eyes are closed and she is off-key. She's silly and intoxicated. She's covered herself with a large fluffy towel while still stretched out on her chaise. Jeff's gone inside to shower and dress.

(If only I were there! Jeff has left the black garbage bag at the side of the barbecue. Unguarded! I'd be having a field day with the leftovers! Of course, if I choked on a chicken bone neither of those two would have noticed, being too busy drinking and listening to that dorky seventies music.)

Carrying mugs full of hot coffee and a bottle of Jameson whiskey on a tray, Sam approaches the sliding glass door.

"'Waterloo!'" he sings loudly, trying to wriggle his hips like he did when he was much younger.

He hasn't noticed that the glass door between the house and the pool area is shut.

(Furthermore, I'm not there to dash over, bark and warn him!)

He smashes into the glass and there's an awful splintering noise.

The glass shatters into a million pieces as Abba sings on without him: "Waterloo!!!!"

CHAPTER 20

Jeff stands on one foot, then the other, in front of the Godots' house. Wary of the stranger, Mrs. Harper looks over at him suspiciously, dogs yanking on their leashes.

Breathlessly, Jeff asks, "Excuse me, ma'am, have you seen Minnie Godot? Either of the Godot kids?"

Mrs. Harper scrunches her face, stares up at him.

"Minnie who? Like Minnie Mouse?"

Just as she says this, Minnie and Danielle drive up and step out of the car. Minnie is carrying Danielle's skateboard, and totally fed up with the baby carrier, Danielle's got Flopsie in her arms.

The dogs spot Danielle and rush towards her, almost pulling Mrs. Harper over. Shocked by the lunging dogs, Flopsie flinches in panic and Danielle turns away.

"Guys. Guys! Calm down!"

Jeff has rushed up to Minnie and he grabs her shoulder. "Don't be upset. It's all right. He's not hurt bad."

Danielle and Minnie (and Flopsie) are frightened and freeze.

"Who's not hurt bad?"

Before Jeff can reply, Danielle squeals, "Oh, my God, it's Dad!!!"

"He's on the porch. I patched him up but -" Jeff explains.

"Sam?" Minnie whimpers.

Mrs. Harper pulls her dogs out of the way of Danielle and Minnie charging the house.

Sam is stretched out on the rattan sofa inside the porch. Tape and gauze decorate his face, arms, hands and legs. A long Band-aid crosses the swollen bridge of his nose that is black and blue, and there's blood on his shirt. Danielle lets Flopsie go free. Her legs are rubbery, and she mutters, "Dad!"

Sam laughs with bravado. "It's okay. Just a few scratches. I had my very own doctor in attendance."

"I've been meaning to put a sticker on that glass door," Jeff stammers, upset. "Thank god it's tampered safety glass, really, I ..."

Minnie pales and sinks down next to Sam. Even Flopsie stares at Sam with shining eyes, then drops some pellets and hops off.

"I'm fine. I'm an ox. Nothing can hurt me."

He flexes an arm muscle.

When she was smaller, Danielle would have squeezed it, but now she doesn't. Instead, she climbs the stairway two steps at a time, slams the door behind her. From the top shelf of her closet she pulls down a red duffle bag and throws it on her bed and starts to fill it with clothes.

CHAPTER 21

"What made you change your mind?" Nicky asks when he opens the front door to let Danielle in.

She tosses her red duffle bag on the floor.

"Your mother's meatballs. You did say you're having spaghetti and turkey meatballs for dinner tonight, didn't you?"

"We have them every Saturday night. We're Italian, remember? Doesn't anyone in your family know how to make meatballs?"

"Probably. But they never do. It's a lot of microwave left-overs these days."

"Ew."

"Yeah. Tell me about it!"

They pass through the living room in which everything is white. Nicky's father and mother are in the hallway, wearing tennis whites and carrying tennis rackets. They greet Danielle affectionately. Nicky's mother inquires, "Have you had any luck with the signs you and Nick posted about your lost dog?"

"Not yet," Danielle answers.

"He was -"

"SHE," Danielle corrects.

"She? But I thought the dog's name was Beckett."

"Yes, it was … is."

"That is usually a name for a -"

"I know that. But I'm not into 'usually.'"

"Well, as I was about to say, she - that dog of yours - sure had, I mean, has a lot of personality."

"She sure did … does. I miss her every day," Danielle confesses.

"Don't give up. She's probably out there looking for you, too."

"Do you think so?"

"No doubt she misses you just as much. Have you offered a reward?" Nicky's practical father interjects.

Danielle makes a mental note to add a reward to the signs around town.

Nicky's mother adds, "Oh, and maybe Nicky's told you but we've decided that he's ready for a dog or maybe two dogs -"

Nicky's father finishes his wife's sentence, "- so keep your eyes open when you visit those rescue places looking for Becker."

"BeckETT. And I will," Danielle promises.

Nicky's parents leave to play tennis at the local courts.

"And I want a big dog. Not a small one," Nicky tells her as they wander into the kitchen. A pot of meatballs and spaghetti are on the stove, and plates, napkins and forks set out on the table. Nicky sticks his finger into the spaghetti sauce and tastes it.

While he adds a little more salt to the sauce and turns on the gas to heat it up, Danielle makes her way into his bedroom. There's a teepee set up in the middle of his room, a drum-set and dozens of glow-in-the-dark stars and galaxies spangling the ceiling. Danielle stares at the new drum - it's a large bass drum that dwarfs all the others. Every year there's a new drum added to the set. She knows because she's known him since the first one - she gave it to him on his sixth birthday. She and Nicky have been sleeping over at each other's places since then, and though girls her age don't usually sleep at boys' houses anymore, she doesn't see why she should stop just because of peer pressure. She likes to do things and discuss stuff that never really interested other girls or boys in her class, who mostly just talk about clothes, celebrities or sports. Danielle prefers skateboards and tree-houses and four-legged-friends. And so does Nicky. Besides, she never had a girlfriend who meant as much to her.

She twirls the drumsticks and bangs on the new drum a few times and slams the cymbals, too. Then she beats away on all the drums in a bit of a frenzy.

It feels good.

She's had enough and puts the drumsticks down.

"Hey, can we eat in the teepee?" she asks when Nicky arrives.

"They never care where I eat, just as long as I eat everything on my plate. AND don't make a disgusting mess."

Danielle smiles. It's nice to be in a calm, peaceful place, even if there are no pets around to liven things up.

"My dad had an accident," she blurts out.

"What do you mean?"

"He walked into a glass door. Maybe his nose is broken. Maybe just bent."

"How come he didn't see it?"

She has no answer. She puts her red bag on one of the two single beds in the room, the one by the window. It has a yellow checked bedspread on it and two fluffy pillows. Then she ducks down to enter into the tent.

"Hey, Dude, don't forget," Nick reminds her.

Danielle bends down to untie her shoelaces, remembering that shoes aren't allowed inside the tent.

"What, are you guys Hindu or something?" she jokes as she flicks her shoes off, one banging on the bass drum when it lands and the other kicking Superman's face on a poster.

"No. I just don't wanna mess up my tent."

"It was my father who taught me how to tie shoelaces," she comments as they settle down onto the tent floor. "If it wasn't for him, I couldn't wear sneakers."

"Oh, wait. How stupid!" Nicky quickly rises up.

"What?"

Nicky stiffens his body and shoots his arms straight out in front of him and wriggles in convulsions, rolling his eyes and dribbling out the side of his mouth, moaning like a zombie.

"Food! Food!" he groans. "We forgot to get dinner! Me, hungry!"

They wriggle out of the tent and head back to the kitchen, both walking with stiff legs and arms like zombies.

CHAPTER 22

While Danielle is away at Nicky's, Sam follows Minnie's repeated request and goes to go see their doctor to check out the wounds on his face. Dr. Prabu has been the family doctor for years, and he doesn't mind opening his office for a weekend visit from Sam. He has very thick, black hair on his head, even though his mustache is almost white. He came from India long ago, and still speaks with a sing-song accent that makes everyone smile. He is not a dog lover and instead keeps a tank of small black asp snakes as his pets near his desk.

(Ugh. Disgusting, I say! Try to cuddle a snake!)

The snake-loving doctor lifts the Band-aids and bandages off Sam's face and peers at the wounds, some still oozing.

"Hmm. That glass sure must have shattered. You're very lucky, Sam."

"Safety Glass," Sam jokes.

"So, tell me how it happened? I mean, REALLY how?"

"Well, Doc, I sorta walked into a glass door."

The doctor gets bandages and disinfectant from a cabinet.

"Nobody 'sorta' walks into a door, Sam. While you're taking off your shirt tell me what's up? By the way, do you have a winning football team this year?"

He begins to clean the wounds one by one using cotton and disinfectant.

"Can't really tell yet. Our next game is on Friday night. I'd love it - ouch! - if you came."

"Sorry. How are Minnie, the kids?"

"Ah, Minnie can be irritable, ready to jump on all of us – ouch!"

"Sorry."

"And Dani … I wish I were either a dog or a rabbit so I could get some affection from her these days."

(If dogs could talk and I was there, I would say, "Why don't you tell him why Danielle's in a bad mood, Sam? Why don't you tell him you abandoned her favorite pet? Me! And while you're at it, why don't you tell him that his asps need a larger tank?")

After cleaning each injury and covering it with a fresh Band-aid, he puts on his stethoscope and listens to Sam's heart. Next, he wraps a blood pressure strap around Sam's upper arm.

"Hey?" Sam replies. "It's my face that got slammed!"

"Sam. Your last physical didn't go as well as I'd have liked. Remember?"

He pumps up the strap and peers closely at the gauge as the numbers appear.

"And that little boy of yours, Simone? How is he doing?"

"Little! He's nearly nine, and going on thirty. And it's Simon."

Dr. Prabu removes the strap and puts his arm around Sam's shoulder.

"What's troubling you, Sam?" he whispers, looking into Sam's eyes. "Anything you say is just between you and me."

Sam's face softens.

"It's hard to pin down. I … I can't seem to remember stupid things - an appointment for a haircut, my car keys, whether or not I brought home olive oil after Minnie's asked me to. Odd things keep happening around the house, too."

("They sure are!" I would say. "And YOU are usually at the center of them, Sam Godot. HELLO!")

"I'll prescribe something to relax you if you like," the doctor offers, watching Sam put his shirt back on and button it. He doesn't like the blood pressure he's just taken, it's too high. Then he notices a purple scorch mark on Sam's wrist.

"Hey, where'd you get that? Broken glass didn't do that."

There is a mystified expression on Sam's face as he examines the mark.

"I don't know. Looks like a burn. But I can't remember it happening. See, that's just the sort of weird stuff I mean."

CHAPTER 23

The new week starts. As usual for Sam, Monday seems like the longest day of the week. When classes and practice are finally finished, he and Rex walk over to the local sidewalk café and take a corner table under the awning. The adjoining tables are crowded with high school kids drinking Cokes and eating fries.

An order of gooey nachos and pitcher of draft beer are delivered by the waitress. She's Latisha, a former student of theirs, and one of the school's best athletes. Recognizing them both, she smiles as she walks away.

Sam stuffs a few chips dripping with hot cheese into his mouth.

"I hate Monday," he comments, his mouth full.

Gesturing toward the Band-aids, and Sam's swollen, black and blue nose, Rex probes, "You sure you weren't run over?"

"Nope. Small plane crash."

Sam laughs at his own joke, but Rex doesn't see the humor.

"Seriously, what happened? You look awful."

Latisha puts two glasses on the table and fills them both from the pitcher. Sam sucks the foam off the top of his glass, still amused.

"Funniest thing that's ever happened."

"Yeah, sure. Ha. Ha. Ha," Rex quips.

"You had to be there. I was attacked by one of those glass patio doors."

Rex winces. Sam rolls his eyes as he recounts: "I was minding my own business and this glass door jumped in front of me, out of nowhere."

Rex finally smiles.

"Think there's a message in this somewhere?" wonders Sam.

"People with glass doors shouldn't ... what?"

"Throw stones? Stow thrones? I think it's time for a change of scene."

"I keep telling you to take your sabbatical like I did last year. Give yourself a real change of scene."

Sam scratches his chin and empties his glass.

"I'm sure you're right. More beer?"

"Nah, I better head home."

"I gotta go, too, but I think I'll just top off my glass. Such a blue sky up there!!"

After Rex has gone, Sam gets a refill and chats with Latisha. She's concerned about the Band-aids on his face, too. He asks about her surfing life since he recalls that she was also a great surfer. She leaves when another customer signals her and Sam finishes the beer. Whistling, he gets up, drops a large tip on the table, stretches and starts walking home.

He has almost passed Surf Travel Agency when he changes his mind, turns around and goes inside. Posters of the Great Wall in China and the Taj Mahal in India and Machu Picchu in Peru decorate the walls of the office. Max Katz, the owner, with a new tattoo of a train encircling his neck, is just putting on his leather jacket in order to leave. Sam greets him with a friendly slap on the back.

Max is perplexed, but then shocked by Sam's injuries.

"Don't be frightened," Sam says. "I'm not a zombie."

"But -"

"Small plane crash."

Sam laughs at his own lame joke.

"So how are you doing?" Sam asks.

Max tilts his head, confused.

"Since, ah, when are you talking to me?"

"Since always. Why?"

"You totally ignored me a few weeks ago, snubbed me in broad daylight."

Sam thinks he's kidding.

"I was on my motorcycle coming up Main Street. You were coming down." Max adds, "I stopped to say Kalimera ...? You acted like you'd never seen me before."

"Must have been my double," Sam jokes. "There are many of me, you know. Some better than others."

"Believe me, it was you," Max insists.

"Well, I haven't been myself lately ... low-grade depression or something. I see you got a new tattoo, goes all around your neck. Must have hurt like hell."

"Yeah, but worth it. My favorite travel mode - the train. After the motorcycle, that is. Pretty cool, eh?"

"Sure is. No pain, no gain, that's what I always tell my players. You've got guts."

Max takes a seat behind his desk.

"So, what's up? What can I do for you?"

"What I need is ... a trip."

Max looks suspicious.

"We've planned so many fantasy trips before, Sam … quite honestly, I'm beginning to think you're not in your right mind."

"I'm for real. I mean, this is for real. I'm … we're going. Honest."

Max goes to his file cabinet, takes out a fat file folder. He spreads out the contents on his desk.

"You prefer the old fashioned way," Sam says, gesturing to the file.

"Yea, I only use a computer when I absolutely have to. Now…It was the Greek tour you wanted, right?"

"Mmm. I just wanna get lost on some little island. Listen, if you can book us, I'll know for sure within the next few weeks if I can take a sabbatical. I want to surprise my wife and kids."

(Boy, am I glad I'm not there to register my disappointment! Greece?! That's, like, FAR! Not a place you can take a dog, the family pet, moi! My idea of a holiday is camping for a week on the river nearby, like we used to do, all together, as a family. Greece! Phooey!)

When Max looks skeptical, Sam squeezes his shoulder.

"Trust me!"

Max isn't sure about that.

"And, hey, cute kids you've got," he comments as he adds the folder to a work pile on his desk.

Now it's Sam's turn to be perplexed.

"That day when I saw you, you were with two kids. They're yours, right?"

"Yeah ... yeah, sure," Sam admits. "But really, I don't remember that at all."

"That's a bit worrying, dude. You don't remember where you were a few days ago and you want to go get lost in Greece?"

CHAPTER 24

It's been a long day and school has finally let out. Nicky's out front in an Iron Man T-shirt waiting for Danielle. He's trying, without success, to do a No-Comply with his skateboard. He cant get it to make a full 180 degree turn, but patiently tries again and again.

One foot on her skateboard, Danielle watches him from a distance, not wanting to approach while he's looking so clumsy. When he rights himself, she skates over.

He tells her: "My grandma gave me fifteen dollars. Let's get some pizza."

"YESSSSS!"

"Before or after we visit the shelter?" he wonders.

"After. Please!"

They skateboard off in the direction of the local animal shelter to check out the dogs in residence in case the right dog has appeared for Nicky to adopt and, as usual and most importantly, to look for Beckett. It's the place where she first found Beckett, and the thought of that makes her shiver when they enter.

(I'd like to tell them not to waste their time, that it's not the shelter I'm in. But I wish it were - I could sure go for some pepperoni pizza!)

After they've checked every cage and open play area and talked to the staff, they skate over to Joe's Pizzeria, their favorite, mostly because of the free refills on drinks.

Seeing them enter, skateboards under their arms, Joe begins preparing their favorite pie, the one they have every time they come in. Standing at the counter, Danielle gulps down a 7 Up and Nicky devours a root beer. They turn to face each other, belch loudly in unison, then giggle and grab refills to carry to their favorite table beside the window.

"Why do they call it root beer when it's not even beer?" Danielle wonders.

"Yeah, weird, huh? I never thought of that," Nicky replies after a particularly slurpy sip.

"I mean, you can drink all you want and it doesn't make you weird, or do stupid things."

They talk about the horrible homework they have to do that evening, and before too long Joe delivers a sizzling hot pizza to the table. Danielle grabs a bubbling slice and tries to take a bite, but is forced to put it back down because she's burnt her tongue. She gulps soda to cool off.

"You're too impatient … about everything these days. What's with you?" Nicky wonders. "And your hair, it's getting like all cave-womany."

"I told you, I'm not touching my hair until I find Beckett," she insists after sipping her drink.

"Your dad acting weird again?" Nicky asks, blowing on a slice.

"I don't ask you why your dad and mom always wear white, do I?"

"Yeah, but my dad doesn't play loud music late at night and jump up and down singing along with old CDs wearing only underwear."

"Please, don't remind me. I can't believe he's my dad," she admits, covering her face with her hands. "I mean, I can believe he's my dad now, today … but not then, not that night. It's like another person is inside him and I don't know that guy … and I don't WANNA know that guy!"

The pizza has cooled enough for her to fold a slice lengthwise and take three bites in a row.

Nicky folds his, too, but nibbles rather than gulps.

(And me, if anybody cares to ask, I'm over here in my cage drooling. DROOLING! I know where Danielle is right at this moment and I know what she is doing - I can almost taste the pizza as she eats. Ooh - I hope that means I'm not going to get gas afterwards like she always does after gulping fizzy drinks! God, I miss Dani's burps! When is this agony ever going to end?)

PART TWO

THE NOT QUITE SO INVISIBLE ELEPHANT

CHAPTER 25

One of the traditions of the Godot family is to sometimes dine on Sunday nights at Zorba's, a Greek restaurant in the next town. It's Sam's favorite place, and tonight it's crowded. Waiters and waitresses are rushing about delivering drinks and Greek specialties to tables covered with pale blue and white cloths, the colors of the Greek flag.

Danielle has pulled up her chair beside Simon. She's helping him with his English homework - grammar - which he hates. They're both glum since she's broken the news to him that, as of her most recent thorough search of the animal shelters, there's still no sign of Beckett.

She's starting to wonder if she will ever see her beloved dog again.

Also, on the way home she fell off her skateboard and sliced a gash near her elbow that's wrapped with gauze. The tumble has her worried - she is not used to getting hurt.

A fresh Band-aid still covers Sam's deepest wound. Most have already healed. In the month since the accident, the bruises on his nose have turned from black and blue to magenta, brown and yellowish. Tonight there is a tantalizing smile on his face, and Minnie notices.

"You're like the cat that's swallowed the canary. You've got a secret, Sam. Can't you just give us a hint?"

Danielle purses her lips, "A cat wouldn't swallow a canary. That's a silly thing to say, Mom."

"Yeah, it would chomp it up in small pieces!" Simon grins.

Constantino, the Greek waiter, places a complimentary platter of Greek appetizers on their table. Simon reaches over and points at a pink-colored dip.

"What's that one made of? I always forget."

"It's fish roe. That's eggs, Simon," Danielle explains, "and it tastes salty and creamy. I'm sure you'll hate it, you always do."

To show off her worldliness, Danielle breaks off a piece of pita bread, dips it in the pink spread, and eats it with relish. She dips again and holds it out for Simon who, despite his disgust at the idea of eating pink fish-egg mush, takes a nibble. She's surprised he goes for it - must be getting braver with age - and despite the fishy smell, he finds it tasty.

Constantino slaps Simon on the back, "Bravo!" and walks away.

"Flopsie might like to try this. Pickle, never," Simon comments.

"No, she wouldn't, even though she eats bugs," Danielle reminds him.

"Why not? There's no dead animals in this."

"Eggs, Simon, are pre-animals, or future animals - same thing," Danielle explains smugly.

A Bouzouki player strums a romantic Greek song on the small stage at the front of the restaurant. Minnie leans back into her chair.

Danielle gazes at a small scar on her father's nose.

"To think, Dad, you could have pierced your brain with glass when you walked through that glass door!"

Minnie leans forward in her chair. "And to think we were cursing you for not showing up on the pier that night. I still feel guilty."

Sam puts his arm around her and pours wine into her glass. She stops him as he pours.

"I still remember 'retsina' wine from our honeymoon," she reminisces. " It tastes -"

Sam adds, "- and smells -"

"- like kerosene," they say at the same time, sharing the happiness of days long gone. The reach over and kiss.

Danielle turns away and grumbles.

Simon leans over and takes a sniff from his mother's glass.

"Smells like shoe polish."

Sam laughs. Reaching across the table, he pours a finger or two of wine into Simon's glass and the same amount into Danielle's glass.

Minnie's shocked.

"Sam, they're too young!"

He brushes her off. "It's a special occasion. It won't hurt them."

Curious, Danielle takes a taste of the wine. She isn't sure if she likes it or not. It certainly has a strange, medicine-like flavor along with a pungent odor. She tastes it again.

Simon ignores the wine. Having gathered his courage, he's busy tasting appetizers, one after the other, while Sam refills his now empty glass and raises it in a salute.

"Dani, Simon, Minnie ... I'm a happy man tonight."

Their orders are brought - a platter of juicy lamb chops, Greek salad, roasted potatoes with oregano and lemon. Lamb chops are Danielle's favorite dish, and she digs in.

Constantino joins the bouzouki player on the stage. He begins a Greek folk dance, slow and bouncy. The metallic music is infectious and diners start clapping to the beat.

After eating several lamb chops, a few potatoes, some salad and drinking a few more glasses of wine, Sam begins to clap noisily but out-of-tempo to the music. Several customers turn to look. Simon shrinks down in his chair. Danielle tastes the wine in her glass again and feels a little dizzy.

Overflowing with energy, Sam pushes his chair back from the table and stumbles over to join Constantino on the stage. Putting his arm over Constantino's shoulder, he attempts to join in the Greek dance. But he is clumsy and missing all the steps.

"Make him stop, Mom, please!" Danielle begs her mother. Simon looks around and says, "Hey, everybody's watching Dad. Oh, God!"

Taking a deep breath, Minnie rises and dances up to Sam, linking arms with him. Through a frozen smile she whispers, "Sit down, Sam. You're way out of step."

He shakes off her arm, stumbles, hisses into her ear, "You want to dance - you dance!" and walks away, leaving Minnie foolishly alone on the dance floor with Constantino, who dances on obliviously.

Danielle wishes she could slither down under the table. Or better yet, get on her skateboard and whiz off and … disappear.

CHAPTER 26

Back home, curled up in bed, Danielle is wide awake. The blanket has fallen to the floor and she's chilled, but too disgusted to get up and put it back.

In his room across the hall, Simon is not asleep either. He's straight as a stick, blanket neatly stuffed under his chin. Flopsie is at his side, a few droppings on either side of her.

"Pell-pell," he thinks to himself, and wishes he could smile about poo-labels, but can't. Like Danielle, he didn't like seeing his dad like that.

Sam has fallen asleep and snores loudly on the old rattan couch on the porch downstairs. There is loud music coming from a CD - Greek folk music that's a lot like the music at Zorba's restaurant.

Wrapped in her robe, Minnie tip-toes out onto the porch carrying a blanket. She pauses to right a tipped empty glass and spreads the blanket over Sam. Staring down at him her eyes start to water.

Danielle appears at the doorway clutching a stuffed raccoon that she used to carry all the time when she was younger, but hasn't touched in years. Simon's right behind her, carrying Flopsie. He's sleepy, but doesn't want to be left out.

The CD comes to an end and at last there is silence.

"Mom, how ...." Simon starts to speak.

Minnie raises her finger to her lips and gestures for the kids to follow her into the kitchen.

Once there, Minnie pours hot milk and cocoa powder and sugar into a saucepan, turns on the fire and begins to stir with a wooden spoon. Simon sits morosely in a chair at the kitchen table, cuddling Flopsie. Danielle reaches into the bird cage and Pickle jumps on her fingers. She pets his small head with the back of her finger while he stares at the saucepan, waiting for the cocoa to boil. Pickle hopes they'll give him a taste since it smells so awfully good.

"Why didn't you stop him, Mom?" Danielle gets the courage to say. "He's the coach and everyone knows us. I mean, the whole restaurant laughed at him."

Minnie bristles.

"That's pretty harsh, Dani."

Danielle looks at her accusingly. She's irked that her mom seems to have switched sides, and pets Pickle even harder.

"You always stick up for him even though he's acting crazy," she accuses.

Pickle squawks as if to agree, but maybe it's because he doesn't like such rough caresses.

The cocoa bubbles over and Minnie jumps up and turns off the fire. She pours a cup for each of them and one for herself, and sits down. They are all silent. Simon sets Flopsie on the floor and takes a carrot from the refrigerator and hands it to the rabbit, who lopes off to a corner to munch. Danielle shakes her finger so Pickle will jump back on his perch. He does.

She pokes her finger into the cocoa in case it's too hot. Minnie's about to tell her that she should wash her hands after holding the bird, but decides it best not to at the moment. They've had a rough day.

Pickle chirps, hoping someone will notice he likes cocoa, too. Realizing just that, Simon fills a small saucer with cocoa and places it on the bottom of Pickle's cage.

The carrot is too thick and Flopsie is having trouble gnawing at it, so Minnie gets up to cut it into smaller slices. She notices a knife wrapped in silver tape on the counter. Hoping no one will notice, she quietly pulls off the sticky tape and slices the carrot down to eatable pieces. But Danielle has noticed, and the color drains from her cheeks.

"Your daddy's been under a strain," Minnie tries to explain. "You guys are too young to understand, so be patient with him … and me. We'll be our old selves again, you'll see. C'mon, drink your cocoa."

Simon sips the velvety cocoa, his forehead furrowed. Tears slide down Dani's cheeks like they used to when she was younger. Her mother turns away and twists a dishtowel into the shape of a pretzel, like the knot she feels in her gut. If only there were something she could say or do to make things like they used to be.

Pickle moves from the lower perch to the upper one. He doesn't like it that Danielle's crying, and the cocoa is too gooey on his beak. Soon, he knows, he'll be left alone in the dark with the sound of the water: drip, drip, drip.

(And nobody says a word about me! Not a word! Like I don't exist anymore. Like they don't notice I am not under the table at their feet where I should be/could be/would be if I were there.

I guess they have even heavier things on their mind these days than a missing dog.)

CHAPTER 27

Halloween has just passed. Danielle and Nicky dressed up as vampires since they were getting sick of zombies, just to get some free candy. Simon was Legolas, though the tights were itchy. It used to be everyone's favorite holiday, but somehow the thrill is not what it once was so they came back to Nicky's early from trick-or-treating and watched a scary movie on TV about a rabid dog attacking its family.

(Awful premise for a story! Would never happen! We dogs ADORE our owners and would never hurt them, rabid or not. Frothy mouth and bulging eyes and snarling away, we would rather go for the local cat population or some obnoxious yapping poodle, or even a squirrel. But our owners? Never! Films often lie!)

A week before, the clocks had all been turned back. So, although it is only five in the afternoon, the kitchen is now as black as it would be at midnight and Pickle perches silently in the dark, hoping someone will turn on the light. No one does, and the night seems long indeed, even for a patient Buddhist.

The next day is Saturday, no school, and Danielle begins the day by practicing new flips with her skateboard out in front of the house after breakfast. She tries over and over the same 180 degree turn flip that Nicky had been practicing, and is just as unsuccessful. Many times she ends up sprawled on the sidewalk rather than back on the skateboard. A scrape on her knee oozes a little blood, but she ignores it.

She hears the sound of other skateboard wheels, and looks down the block where Nicky is racing toward her. She makes a mental note that he is getting more confident on his skateboard – she'd better do more practicing to stay ahead of him. When he reaches her, he stops the skateboard but keeps one foot on it.

"Hey. Glad you could come. Follow me. Oh, and hold your nose," she tells him.

She leads him through Mrs. Harper's back yard, both pinching their nostrils shut. The Dobermans bound toward them, two jump on Danielle, one sniffs Nicky's pant cuff.

"Talk to these guys while I go in and get their leashes," Danielle tells him. "Let them smell you all they want, that's how they get to know you."

At the door she shouts, "Mrs. Harper?"

Mrs. Harper is standing at the kitchen table dunking a tea bag into a china cup. Seeing Danielle she says, "Hi, dear," and asks, "Have you seen my glasses?"

Danielle shakes her head.

"Could you help me find them? I bought a few extra pairs, I think. But ... where do they go?"

Danielle sees a pair of glasses on top of the toaster. She hands it to Mrs. Harper.

"Is It Okay If My Friend And I Take The Dogs For A Run?" she asks loudly.

"It's better than okay. They'd love it. Poor things are so bored with old me ..." her eyes search the kitchen, "If you can find their leashes, that is."

Danielle walks into the living room. Right away she spots the leather leashes hanging over Mrs. Harper's old fashioned TV. She also sees three pair of reading glasses on the couch, two on top of the TV under the leashes, and one pair is balanced over a doorknob.

Back in the garden, Nicky has let the dogs get to know him with sniffs and licks and leaps. When Danielle returns, she clips a leash to each dog collar. Then she grabs her skateboard, and tells Nick to grab his.

"C'mon."

On the street, she positions herself half-on and half-off her skateboard. Following her lead, Nicky does too. Danielle keeps two dog leashes for herself and hands the third to Nicky.

"Okay, let's go!"

She jiggles the leather strap, and when her two Dobermans begin to trot forward, she lifts her other foot onto the skateboard so the dogs can pull her along. Nicky then does the same. Feeling himself being pulled along, he whoops loudly, "Yaaa-whooo!"

As the road slants downhill they pick up speed - faster, Faster, FASTER!- wheels whirling across the asphalt, multiple furry paws trotting up ahead, tongues hanging out and dog slobber flinging from their snouts.

At the bottom of a dip when the road starts to slants upward, they slow down, and Nicky pulls up alongside Danielle.

"That was SO cool! If only I could have dogs like these for my own …"

"After we've had our ride, we'll stop off at the dog shelter!" Danielle shouts. "Let's try finding you a dog. And maybe, just maybe, Beckett has turned up. I can't stop hoping. Am I a jerk?"

("Sorry, not a chance of finding me there!" I'd like to yell at her. I'm still sulking in this dirty animal shelter far away,

wondering if I will EVER have a family again. I'm starting to have nightmares. Danielle, old pal, do something!)

CHAPTER 28

(It's been over two months since that Most Terrible of Days, otherwise known as Lost-At-The-Park-by-Crazy-Man-Day, and still no sign of me, Beckett. But I saw THEM! The other night I was being walked near the shelter onto a high grassy slope and a car passed that resembled Mr. Godot's, so I looked and there was Danielle and Simon in the backseat. They were looking down in their laps, probably at some stupid video game, so they didn't notice me, and by the time I barked to get their attention, the car had passed. It was heading towards that Greek restaurant they often go to. It made my heart stop to see them after so long, and then stop again when I realized that we came so close to be reunited, that I might have gotten juicy lamb chop bones for supper and that such an opportunity might not happen again. I can't give up hope entirely ... but the nightmares continue.)

After school on Monday, Simon and Jerry walk their mountain bikes toward Simon's home. They're jittery after spending the afternoon taking tests in English grammar and history, not exactly either one's best subjects.

"You signing up for soccer again?" Jerry asks Simon.

"Nnnn ... don't know."

"Why not? The Scout meetings have changed to Thursday night, so it can't be that," Jerry nags. "Besides, it goes towards our Activity Badge."

"Yeah, I know … but my dad forgot to pick me up from two meetings last month. Don't you remember? I can't count on him like before. How will I get home?"

They turn the corner.

Jerry suggests, "Well, maybe my dad can pick you up for the meetings. I mean, I can ask."

Simon's face brightens.

"Well, yea, sure, if you think he won't mind."

Danielle turns the corner, and seeing the boys up ahead she jumps on her board and races towards them. Reaching them she jumps off, and jump-kicks her board up under her arm. Jerry's in the middle of a story.

"- and he was behaving all crazy-like and always forgetting everyday things. My dad couldn't figure out what was wrong. He sent him for tests and it turned out to be a tumor on the brain."

Often Jerry tells Simon the more dramatic cases from the hospital that his father has discussed with the family at the dinner table.

"A brain tumor! Gosh. Did they operate?" Simon replies.

"Nope, it was too late."

"Well, what happened?"

"He died!"

"Wait. You mean a brain tumor can cause forget-fulness?" Danielle interrupts.

"Well, yeah. It's what my dad said."

Danielle puts her skateboard down and points it in the opposite direction before climbing on.

"Hey, aren't you coming home?" Simon asks.

"No, Dad's got a game tonight and Mom's work-ing, so there's no rush to get home."

The boys watch as she rolls away, then start talking about who is more powerful - the Incredible Hulk or Captain America?

Her destination is the public library, an old his-toric building a few blocks away with a brass plaque that says '1876' above the door. Inside the library, she goes to a computer and Googles "Brain Tumor." Soon she's at a table beside the medical section with a stack of books open in front of her, skimming chapters, and scribbling notes on scraps of papers.

Finally she grabs her backpack, leaves the library and skates at top speed over to the high school. On arrival, she puts her skateboard under her arm and hurries to her father's office.

Sam has been pacing around the office. He's sip-ping from a blue bottle of Maalox, and rubbing his troubled stomach when Danielle barges in.

"Buenos Días, Papa."

"Hey! Hola, Dani! Are you coming to the game? Only two hours to go!"

"I wanted to speak to you first," she says gravely. "Dad, I've been to the library doing research, putting together some of the bad stuff that's been happening with you, the forgetting, and ..."

Sam impatiently glances at his watch.

"Dad, this is important. It could help you a lot and explain –"

Sam's cell phone rings and Sam answers, says a few words, closes the phone.

"Wait, Honey, sorry. You wanna HELP me?"

"Yeah, that's what I'm getting at. I've been doing some research, and it's evident -"

Sam interrupts. "Listen, Dani, what I really need more than anything else in the world right now is for you to do something about that ape of a quarterback that West Park High School is about to uncage on us. If you really want to help me, arrange for lightening to strike the goons on the other team...or their bus to blow a tire.."

"But ..."

"If we lose this one we haven't got a shot this season, Dani. It'll kill me!"

"You won't lose, Dad!" she reassures him, hugging him hard before she walks away.

Outside, she hops on her skateboard and rides home in a hurry to enact a plan that's forming in her head. Luckily Simon's there. She asks if she can borrow his bicycle.

"Sure," he says, "if I can have Flopsie two nights in a row!"

Danielle wants the bike so bad, she'd agree to anything at that moment. She goes into the house to get a map from her father's study, grabs it and stuffs it into her back pack. Once outside and speeding along on Simon's bike, she turns onto the busy Coast Road.

Fifteen minutes later she reaches West Park Boulevard where she stops and consults the map. She rides on, looking at street signs until she comes to West Park High School, stopping first at a corner shop for a Sprite since the ride has made her really thirsty.

A lady outside stands beside a box of free puppies, and Danielle doesn't even notice.

CHAPTER 29

Dropping her bike in West Park High's parking lot beside the yellow team bus, Danielle kneels down beside one of its big wheels. Looking around to make sure nobody is nearby, she unscrews the tire cap, takes a pen out her pocket and pushes it down into the valve. Air starts to escape with a hiss. After the tire has gone flat, she goes to the next tire and does the same, then over to the third tire.

At the fourth tire, Danielle glances left and sees a large pair of scuffed leather shoes stop at her side. Then she hears a deep voice from high above her say, "Okay, Kid, stand up nice and slow."

When she does, she's facing a large, grizzled security guard who has a gun in a holster and meaty arms and legs.

"Oops!" she mutters.

CHAPTER 30

Inside the smelly locker room, standing on a bench, Sam gives his football team a pep talk as the players huddle around him.

"Alright, listen up! It takes two to tango, boys, and we ain't going to dance nicely. Right?"

In unison the team shouts: "RIGHT!"

"We're down, but we're not out. Right?"

"RIGHT!!"

"I know we can do it. Right?"

The players shout even louder.

"RIGHT!!!"

Sam turns to a huge player who has a shaved head with a tattoo of a tiger on his skull.

"Do me a favor, Tinkerton, don't think. JUST RUN!"

He approaches the players one by one, rubbing each head for luck. "Okay, boys. Go do it!!!"

The players run past him and out of the locker room. Sam follows. As each appears on the field, the Limerick fans in the stands stamp, whistle and cheer. The visiting West Park fans hiss and boo.

Sam and his team sit side-by-side on their bench. The visiting team has yet to arrive, and even after some time, their bench remains empty. Sam looks at his watch and shakes his head in disbelief. The crowd is puzzled, too, and is getting restless. The home team's cheerleaders are sent out and start to do a routine to fill up time, but the fans start booing.

Then popcorn starts flying. Then cups of ice. For the next half hour food and taunts are tossed into the air.

Finally, the West Park players run out onto the field, nearly an hour late. Their fans stand up and cheer and grunt and stomp their feet.

And the game begins.

(Okay, I know this is inappropriate, but I gotta make a comment here. It's about sports. Human sports. You guys take it waaaay too seriously. We dogs, we run and play and chase balls same like you, but it is all in fun. F-U-N. But you humans, you act like it's the end of the world if you lose the ball, or worse, lose the game. And worse still, you act all aggressive if a team you follow loses. Not YOU losing personally, but OTHER people! From a dog's point of view, where it is all about the thrill-of-the chase, that just seems rather lame. End of comment.)

CHAPTER 31

First thing the next morning, Danielle sits nervously on a bench outside of the principal's office. She has never been in trouble like this, and trembles with fear and embarrassment.

She thinks of her father. And she thinks of Beckett.

(About time! I can tell when she is thinking of me, and it's been a couple days of No-Beckett-Thoughts. And I presumed she could never live without the smell of my ears.)

Finally the door opens. The principal, Valerie Price, a nimble silver-haired woman wearing a cream-colored suit, stands in the doorway. There's a severe look on her face.

Danielle follows her into the office and sits at the edge of a chair in front of the large desk while Mrs. Price remains standing, hands on her hips.

"Danielle, I'm utterly surprised by what you did. An act of hooliganism like that. You of all people, with your good grades, who was certainly brought up to be fair-minded in sports. It just doesn't seem like you."

"I'm sorry, Mrs. Price, I wasn't thinking straight." Under her breath she mutters, "A lot of good it did. Dad's team lost anyway!"

"Excuse me! It might have been a fiasco if the other team hadn't been able to refill the tires and get to the game."

Mrs. Price folds herself into the chair behind the desk.

"I don't understand. Didn't you realize that it would have come down on your father if the game had to be cancelled because of this? Why, if he were my dad - the coach, a good father - I'd idolize him."

"But I ... I ... wouldn't hurt my father. I was trying to HELP him."

"Help him?"

"You don't understand ... he HAD to win, Mrs. Price. He just had to! And now that he hasn't, I don't know what will ..." Danielle stops herself from saying more.

Just then Minnie walks into the office.

"Dani, what's this all about?"

"Mrs. Godot, please, have a seat," Mrs. Price pulls up a second chair.

"No, thank you. This is a family matter and we'll take care of it at home." Minnie clasps Danielle's arm, "Grab your skateboard, honey, and let's go. NOW."

"Mrs. Godot, PLEASE," Mrs. Price insists.

"Thank you for your trouble," is all Minnie replies as she pulls Danielle out of the office and through the corridor.

Once they are gone, Valerie Price picks up the phone and calls an office just down the hall.

"We've got a problem."

CHAPTER 32

The next afternoon, Danielle and Mrs. Price are sitting opposite Amy Benchley, the young guidance counselor at school. Amy Benchley is short and chirpy with little dimples and thick, long auburn hair. She tries to look Danielle in the eye, but Danielle's hair is hanging over her face.

"Hey," she says to get Danielle's attention. "What you did is very wrong, Honey. We need to know why you did it."

Danielle raises her face and there is a mix of anger and confusion in her eyes. The principal notices it, adding, "We're here to help you."

"There's nothing wrong with me. It's me who should be upset! It's me everybody's hiding it from ...!"

"Hiding what?" asks Amy.

"No one's helping him! He needs help!"

Amy's perplexed.

"Her father," Mrs. Price explains. "She thinks we're not helping her father, who is the athletics coach at the high school."

"Of course, Coach Godot. But Danielle, what's wrong with your father? Everyone likes him."

Just then a messenger peeks in the door and summons the principal urgently.

"I'll get back as soon as I can," Mrs. Price promises as she departs.

When they're alone, Amy coaxes Danielle to tell her about her library research.

Amy's eyes widen as she listens. "A brain tumor? Seriously?"

Danielle pulls the various notes she made in the library out of her backpack and strews them across the counselor's desktop. "See, according to my sources ... I looked on the internet, and in medical books in the library... I've concluded that Dad's suffering from a brain tumor, probably inop ... inoper ... can't be operated."

"Honey, I had no idea."

"And no one's helping him."

"But what exactly led you to that precise diagnosis?"

Danielle looks at her notes: "The symptoms they have in common - memory loss or amnesia, sudden morose behavior, mood changes ..." she looks up at Amy, her lips are quivering.

"He must know something's wrong, too. I think he's drinking all that smelly wine and beer that makes him act all weird to cover up the fear he must have. Or the pain ..."

She starts to crumble, "We're losing him! My dad! Meanwhile I've been P.O.'ed at him about some personal things and haven't been nice to him for a long time. And ... and, maybe he's dying!"

Danielle's puts her hands over her eyes. There's no stopping the tears that are leaking through her fingers.

CHAPTER 33

It's the following day and Amy, Danielle and Minnie are gathered in Amy's office.

Danielle reads from the list of symptoms in her notes: "... headaches, accidents, and he's going deaf. I don't know if this is separate or endemic ... if that's the word I copied, en-dem-ic."

Minnie's face is icy. "Dani, honey, I don't see what Sam's health has to do with Miss Benchley. Your dad's a private man."

In a soft voice Amy turns to Minnie, "But Mrs. Godot -"

Minnie cuts her off. "Sam's health is none of anybody's business."

Amy pushes on, anyway. "But Danielle's anxiety IS our concern. Your daughter is disturbed about her father and his true or imagined affliction. Just look at what it's doing to her."

They look over at Danielle who is miserable and pale, her hair a tangled mess. She takes a wadded hankie from her pocket and blows her nose.

Minnie leans back in her chair and sighs deeply. Then takes a deep breath. "For weeks and weeks she's been mad at all of us, especially her dad, about … about her lost dog. But she's never done something so outrageous before. Frankly, I'm shocked. She's a terrific kid."

Minnie's eyes wander to the window and she sighs again, then goes on.

"It's true. Sam hasn't been quite himself lately but it's nothing serious. His -" she stops, starts again, "Our doctor examined him recently. There were some tests."

She leans forward and grabs Danielle's hands. "Honestly, Dani," she reassures, "they couldn't find anything. Some high blood pressure, that's all. Your father's fine."

"And the amnesia?" Danielle asks, pulling her hands away.

"He's forgetful, Danielle. It comes with age."

"What about his hearing?"

"His hearing?"

"You know how he gets, Mom. Late at night, he turns his music on, then louder and louder, like he can't hear it or something."

"Is that so?" Amy asks Minnie.

"Yes," Minnie responds protectively, "but only after he's had a few drinks. He gets, how can I explain … mellow."

"And what about the amnesia?" asks Amy.

"That's an exaggeration. He's gotten a bit forgetful in the past months."

"A bit? What about Beckett?" Danielle challenges her mother. "I'll probably never get over losing Beckett. I think my life is ruined for good!"

(Boy, am I glad to hear that! I mean, that she misses me so much. It may have ruined my life, too.)

Minnie's face reddens. "It was an accident, Dani, c'mon. It could have happened to any one of us."

"What?" asks Amy.

"Oh, Danielle's dad foolishly left our dog Beckett at the dog park and she didn't find her way -"

Danielle cuts in, "He FORGOT our dog in the park, in the sun, near busy streets, with no water, and she … disappeared. Maybe she got hit by a car or something! And when all of us went back the next day to look for her, Beckett was gone."

"Where had he gone when he left the dog?"

"He was at a clambake on the beach," Minnie starts to explain. "His Army reunion -"

"Partying, Mom, partying! And drinking," Danielle cuts in again. "He FORGOT he'd left Beckett in the dog park, then he FORGOT where he left the car and got driven home by someone else. Is that sane? He loves Beckett as much as I do, he'd never hurt her in his right mind. It's not like Daddy. It has to be something like a growth pressing on his brain."

Minnie is embarrassed. She looks at Amy, "He and his friends had a few drinks. Sam hadn't seen his buddies in fifteen years."

She turns back to Danielle. "Oh, come on! You make him sound like a mental defective."

"Was he drinking when he walked into the glass door?" asks Amy.

Minnie's face reddens again.

"Danielle told me about his accident."

"He'd had a few, yeah, sure," Minnie answers. "It was a hot day, you know? A few beers and sun, it'd make anybody a bit - uh -"

"He drank all afternoon with my parents' friends who have a pool and it wasn't just beers, it was those yucky bloody drink thingies," Danielle snarls.

Amy takes a breath before saying, "I take it he drinks a lot?"

"Not a lot," Minnie replies. "Just socially, like most of us."

Danielle averts her gaze and Amy notices.

"Danielle? Tell me. Does he?"

Danielle doesn't look at her, but nods meekly.

"Ah, c'mon, Dani. He never bumps into walls or sings opera at the dinner table like your Uncle Ned," Minnie says, then turns toward Amy. "I mean, he never ACTS drunk. It wouldn't be a big deal if it weren't for the late-night music …"

Amy pushes the pad away. She looks first at Danielle then over at Minnie.

"Why don't you have the situation assessed by people who know how to evaluate these things? The Pacific Institute is very reputable. Harry Harding is a friend of mine. Alcoholism is -"

At the word "alcoholism" Minnie gasps.

Amy continues. "- cunning, baffling, insidious. It's an illness that tells you that you don't have it, and you think you're okay."

Danielle bursts out, "Alcoholism! It's not THAT bad. That's like way worse than a brain tumor. Dad's a coach, not a wino."

Minnie adds, "He's not that bad, really."

"I'm not saying it's that bad. Just check it out," suggests Amy reassuringly.

Minnie ignores the slip of paper with the address that Amy has written on, and instead says, "Sam would be so betrayed, if he knew we were here."

"Please be assured of confidentiality," Amy adds, holding the paper out.

Minnie blinks several times and hesitates.

Danielle reaches out, grabs the paper and stuffs it in her pocket.

CHAPTER 34

Minnie and Danielle drive along the scenic Coast Road in Minnie's small black car. The gray-green ocean sparkles, and scatterings of people walk or sit along the edge of the sandy beaches. They pass a volleyball game. Further down they pass a bunch of surfers trying to catch waves and dogs romping in the sand. Danielle looks carefully but sees that her lost dog is not among them.

As she drives along, Minnie punches the radio from station to station. Danielle alternates between staring out the window and glancing over at her mother expectantly. Normally she would hang out the window as far as possible when any surfers are in view.

The road sign announces Limerick Beach. Minnie turns the radio off as she pulls to the side of the road to stop. She turns to look at Danielle.

"I've got to work tonight, Dani."

"Okay. And? Was that counselor creepy or what? I mean, Dad may have brain problems but … he's not a skid row bum."

"No, he's not. Far from it." She looks at her watch, uncomfortable with the conversation. "Oh, Baby, I'm late. Really, I've got to go. Sorry."

Danielle gets out of the car and watches her mother drive away, grumbling that she's just called her "baby" again. She's a few blocks from home and walks uphill, wishing she had Beckett with her walking back and forth between her sneakers, almost tripping her. Or Nicky. Or her skateboard. Something, anything, to distract her from the anxious thoughts that are swimming around in her head.

Minnie drives on. She turns the radio back on and searches for something that will take her mind off things. Nothing grabs her attention.

Finally she settles on a talk show about the Arctic and climate change.

(Little does she know, but minutes later she's only two streets from the shelter in which I'm being held. I may be getting a change of climate myself; the lady who runs the shelter has let me out of my cage to meet an older man who's looking for a pet to take with him to an Assisted Living Home. I wonder if he wants me to catch sticks or sleep on his feet to keep him warm! Although my mind is open, I sure do wish that Minnie would slow down, turn off the freeway and rescue me. But she doesn't.)

A half hour later Minnie reaches Verdes and parks her car in the small Verdes Ballet School parking lot. Several cars also pull into the lot and little girls and a few boys spill out. The kids are four, five and six years old, each carrying a canvas tote bag containing dance costumes and ballet shoes.

One by one they greet Minnie as she climbs out of her car.

"Hi, Mrs. Godot."

"Hi!"

Inside, while the girls change into tutus and the boys into tights, Minnie sits on the edge of Rosa's desk. Rosa Mesa is the young receptionist who almost always has bright red lipstick on her lips; her eyes are dark and shiny. While Minnie relates the entire incident with Danielle and the counselor, Minnie pulls a cigarette out of her purse, lights it and inhales deeply.

"Hmm. That's not like Danielle to get herself in trouble," Rosa comments. "And look at you. You've been off cigarettes for three years. And now -"

"Little rat!"

"Wow, you're really upset."

"I felt so embarrassed, getting my wrist slapped by a guidance counselor. And her accusing my husband of ugly things. Alcoholism! Who doesn't drink?"

Rosa neither agrees nor disagrees.

The girls and boys have taken their places at the railing in the adjoining rehearsal room. They're not very organized. Minnie joins them and signals Dan, the piano player, to begin warm-up exercises.

The kids do pliés, jumps, arabesques, watching themselves in the mirrored wall.

Irritably, Minnie bangs on the piano, stops the music and shouts.

"NO. NO. NO. Kristina, Charlotte, Tyler. LEGS STRAIGHT. Let's try it again."

The music begins once more. The boy at the end of the line whispers to the girl beside him, "What's with Mrs. Godot? She's being so mean!"

Seeing how unorganized the children still are, Minnie pounds on the top of the piano again. The children have never seen her behave so aggressively.

"LINE UP. LEGS STRAIGHT. WE HAVEN'T GOT ALL DAY."

She turns away for a moment and tries to settle down. Straightening her spine, she turns back to face the class, pretending everything is all right.

CHAPTER 35

A few days later Danielle goes into Mrs. Harper's back yard after school to take the Dobermans for a long walk. She's still a bit shaken from the conferences at school and wants to see the dogs and get cuddles. Overwhelmed by the ever-increasing stink from the poop, she decides to take action.

She goes home, gets a big garbage bag, a clothespin, and finds Simon's camping shovel. Returning with her Anti-Poop Kit, she pinches her nose shut with the clothespin and spends an hour shoveling brown clumps into the garbage bag. When all the piles are gone, she ties the ends of the bag together and – on her way out – drops it into the dumpster.

(Please note: MY poop never smells bad, but more like lavender or fresh roses in spring. But what do you expect from Dobermans?!)

The sun is setting. Unfortunately, it's now too late to take the dogs for their walk. Feeling guilty, Danielle opens the back door just enough for three dog noses to poke out, which she scratches one by one, while rubbing her own nostrils that have gotten sore from being pinched together with the clothespin.

"Sorry, guys," she says as she gently coaxes them back into the house.

Walking home, she turns and notices that the Dobermans are gazing at her through their living room window. Their sad eyes are saying, "What, no walk?!"

(They're stately dogs, I'll admit it, even as they slobber on the window. But three of THEM don't equal one of scruffy ME. I'll bet Danielle is showering them with attention just because she's missing ME!)

Back home, she scoops up Flopsie, and carries her out to the porch.

She ties a tartan plaid ribbon around the rabbit's neck, and holding the long end tries to get it to walk around the porch like a small pet dog. Flopsie is not compliant and tries to go left when Danielle tugs to the right. Sam is already home, sitting on the porch turning pages of the local newspaper and silently watching her. He has his feet up and sips from a can of beer. He goes back to the paper to read an article about the coming basketball season. There's even a photo of him with last year's team, so he tears out the article.

Danielle tires of trying to get languid Flopsie into action and hoists her onto her chest instead, stretching out in the hammock with her World History book, stroking Flopsie's silky fur with her free hand while she reads about Napoleon.

(Meanwhile, if anybody cares, I've just been moved to the Sunrise View Senior Home to assist with all the old folk there - they call it pet therapy. There are a lot of perks - they've put a doggie bed in the corner of a storage room for me, and one of the nurses brought me a bowl of leftover chicken soup my first night and patted my head! Tomorrow I begin my "work" and I'm not sure if I'll like it or exactly what it is I'm to do. A dim-witted parakeet and hare-brained rabbit I know how to deal with, but not old people. What if they don't like me or my half-cut ear and boot me out? I can just tell that this is going to be another sleepless night of worrying.)

Outside the porch windows the gaudy sunset has finished and it's starting to get dark.

Simon suddenly appears in the doorway. His T-shirt has a picture of a soccer ball on it that states "BORN TO KICK."

"Hey, Dad, where's Mom? I'm hungry."

"She has class tonight. Remember?"

"It's Wednesday, Dork." Danielle mutters.

Sam folds the newspaper. "I'm hungry, too. Hey, Si, would you go into the kitchen and see what Mom left us for supper?"

Simon does, and finds a whole chicken in a roasting pan that's defrosted. He shouts, "Chicken!" and seeing small potatoes on the counter beside the chicken, adds, "Roasted potatoes!"

He hadn't noticed the salad in a bowl at the end of the counter, but after Pickle's chirp, he shouts, "And salad!"

Back on the porch, Sam tells the kids, "I don't feel like cooking. Do you?"

Simon gives him a look that says, "Me, neither."

"What say we take a drive? Get some dinner at the pier!"

"YESSSS!" Danielle yells, popping her head up from behind the book.

"But I have tests tomorrow," Simon explains.

"How many?" Sam asks.

"Two.

"What in?"

"Science and math."

"You're great in both."

"Ha!" Danielle snaps.

"Because I study."

"HA!" Danielle remarks even louder.

Sam thinks for a moment. "How's this: we'll go to the pier, make it fast."

He looks at his watch. "It's six-thirty now, I'll have your nose home in a book by eight-thirty. How's that?"

"If his nose is in a book, what about the rest of his head?" Danielle giggles.

"Oh, funny, Dan-Dan!" Simon rolls his eyes.

Sam kneels at Simon's feet and makes begging faces. "Pretty, pretty, pleassssse."

Simon can't resist him. Not needing any persuasion, Danielle has already closed her history book and is lacing up her sneakers. They get ready to go, pausing only long enough for Sam to convince Danielle to leave Flopsie at home.

"Just this once," Sam bargains.

Both kids squeeze into the front seat of Sam's old blue Saab. It takes a few tries to get it started but soon they're tootling along the Coast Road, toward the pier as the last of the sunset turns the horizon a metallic red.

Danielle is squished, but smiling. She hasn't seen her father this giddy in a long time and hopes that it's a sign that things will get back to normal.

CHAPTER 36

It's dark by the time Sam parks in the lot next to the pier. Elated that Danielle is being friendly, he puts an arm around the shoulders of both children while strolling from the parking lot into the seafood restaurant. Sliding into a window booth overlooking the water, they can see the Pacific Ocean below glistening in the moonlight, and brightly lit amusement rides and arcades along the pier reflected in the high tide.

"Order anything you want!" Sam grandly announces.

After a small discussion, the kids order fried clams with lemon and tartar sauce. Sam orders a whole boiled lobster for himself.

Danielle looks out the window and counts the surfers still in the water who are reflected in the lights. Nearly half of them are girls and women, she notices, something that wasn't true when she was little.

Very hungry now, they dig in as soon as their food lands on the table. When the kids are finished, they order ice cream sundaes. Meanwhile, Sam cracks shells and picks every last morsel of food from his lobster.

Red lobster shells pile up beside congealing melted butter and an untouched baked potato. The waitress brings the desserts. Simon had requested an extra cherry and is happy when his sundae arrives with three. Sam orders an Irish coffee - whiskey and coffee and cream.

In a chatty mood, Sam has them giggling with stories about some of the ridiculous moments in games that his teams have played, like when one of his quarterbacks leaned back so far to catch the ball that he made a flip backwards and still caught the ball. And the time their uniforms shrank in the wash and everybody had to give their uniforms to their smaller team-mates, leaving the bigger guys with nothing to wear. And when - Dani's favorite - lightening hit the baseball bat and splintered it.

Bringing Sam's coffee, the waitress makes a show of pouring strong Jameson whiskey into the cup. Simon finishes the last of his melted ice cream, and Danielle's eaten about as much as she can and pushes the half-full plate away. Sam pulls out his wallet and removes a twenty dollar bill with a flourish.

"How about a few rides on the bumper cars?"

Danielle jumps to her feet; Simon is all smiles. They grab the twenty dollars and race out onto the pier. They pass the merry-go-round and the Ferris wheel that are lit up with colored lights. The bumper cars are an old family favorite. They're lit up too, though a few bulbs are burned out, Danielle notices.

Inside the restaurant, the waitress gathers up the dirty plates.

"Nice kids you've got."

"The best. What more could a man want - a full stomach, happy children, a view of the Pacific Ocean … and another Irish coffee."

"Right away, sir."

On the bumper car ride, Danielle and Simon are quickly out of breath from laughing hard as they smack their cars into each other. As soon as the ride ends, they jump back in line. The starter at the gate comments, "You two again?"

As the gate opens, they rush onto the floor and claim their prospective cars - Danielle's is painted yellow, Simon's is black with a red stripe.

CHAPTER 37

Minnie's black car pulls up to the house. She's glad to be home. Lights inside the house blaze out into the dark of night. "Hello, everyone. I'm home," she announces, unlocking the door.

When there's no reply except Pickle's chirp, she drops her purse onto the counter and strolls into the living room. Seeing that it's empty, she peeks into the kitchen. Nobody. But all the food she had left is still there, uncooked. Next she walks upstairs and looks into Simon's silent bedroom.

In Danielle's bedroom she discovers that Flopsie has been left out of the cage and has been nibbling Danielle's shoelaces. A long line of poop pellets are scattered across the floor. She takes a tissue from her pocket, gathers up the poop and drops it in the waste-basket. She walks into hers and Sam's bedroom. It's dark. Turning on the bedside lamp, she sees Sam's clothes scattered across the bed, also his cell phone.

Back downstairs, she's alone, and edgy. She takes kindling from the box beside the fireplace, and, with the cast iron poker, scatters the old ash remaining in the fireplace in order to build a new fire. While poking, she uncovers Sam's half-burned Nike shoe in the charred remains. She pulls it out, stares at it, then - vehemently - throws it back into the fireplace.

"Burn up for all I care," she mutters.

She piles up the kindling, lights a fire, and fans it. When a flame has flared up, she places a piece of driftwood on top.

Soon the fire's roaring. She lights a cigarette and stands at the window.

"Where are they," she wonders? "Is something going on that I've forgotten about?"

CHAPTER 38

Sam leans back in his chair at the restaurant. He's enjoying the blurry site of the colored lights of the merry-go-round and Ferris wheel, and smiles. There's a third Irish coffee in front of him.

Danielle runs into the restaurant rubbing her forehead. "Dad, someone hit me on the head 'cuz I rammed their car. That's against the rules."

Simon rushes up behind her. "Dad, there's a bunch of creeps out there. Can we go now?"

"In just a few minutes, Si. You guys…you guys stayed out so long, I ordered a nightcap." His voice is slurred and erratic and they see that he has that foggy look in his eyes which means Be Careful Or Trouble.

"But, Dad! It's eight-thirty-five. I've got to study. Remember?"

"Don't be such a goody-two-shoes, Simon, my man. I told you … just a few… few minutes more."

He takes out his wallet, removes another $20 bill, but his voice stings Simon.

"Stop thinking about yourself, Si, and act like … a gentleman. Take your sister to the shooting range."

Simon swallows. "But, Dad! You promised!!!"

Sam's irritated now, and defensive too. "Oh, so what, so I sssaid 'around' 8:30. Jeez, Simon, can't we have some fffun? Don't be an old fart."

Simon flings the money down on the table.

"I'm going to sit in the car." He stomps off.

"What a little snot your brother can be."

He hands his daughter the twenty dollar bill. "Here, Dani, have a little tttarget practice and I'll be ready in a minute or two ..."

Danielle's nervous about going back out alone. And the good mood of the evening has soured.

"Won't you shoot with me, Dad?"

"You're my sharpshooter, remember?" He takes a large gulp of his Irish coffee.

She leaves, but without enthusiasm. An eerie boat horn sounds.

Morose, sitting alone in the back seat of the dark car with only the illumination from his cell phone, Simon speed dials.

Danielle stands outside the restaurant for a few minutes not knowing what to do. Not the pretty lights on the pier, not the twenty dollar bill in her hand, not the few surfers remaining, not even thoughts of Beckett's fuzzy face can brighten her anxious mood.

(What? Not even my fuzzy face! Uh, oh ... this is serious. I should be there at her side, licking her fingers or making my Aren't-I-Cute face to get her to smile.)

CHAPTER 39

At the house, the phone rings. As Minnie listens to Simon's words, the color drains from her cheeks.

She hangs up and in one sharp move strides over to the small family bar. Carrying bottle after bottle into the kitchen, she dumps the contents of each down the sink and throws the empties into the recycle bin.

Next she pulls open the refrigerator door so aggressively that two fridge magnets - one of a four-leaf clover, one a photo of Beckett - fly off. She tosses beer cans in the garbage while Pickle looks on.

And the only sound now is the eerie drip, drip of the broken faucet.

CHAPTER 40

At the shooting gallery, Danielle shoots at targets. Or tries to. She misses nearly every shot, and that's rattling her even more.

"UGH!" she grunts, and stomps over to pay for more shots.

The crowd on the pier is a bit rougher now that it's later at night. An older girl takes some quarters from Danielle's change on the counter. Seeing the tattoo of a devil on her cheek, Danielle hurries back to shoot some more, but her legs are rubbery, her head all dizzy, and she is getting more and more fed up with this family drama.

(Oh Gosh! I REALLY should be there! Just a rub of my head against her leg or a look of sweetness in my eyes could change her mood in an instant.

We are not called Man's Best Friend for nothing.)

CHAPTER 41

Minnie, watches the fire and listens to the news on the radio, glancing down every now and then at her watch..

In the kitchen, the defrosted chicken remains untouched on the counter while Pickle stares into the darkness. He is very tense, not liking the situation at all.

The fridge magnet of Beckett is nowhere to be seen on the floor.

The four-leaf clover one has broken in half.

CHAPTER 42

Sam speeds unsteadily away from the pier along the Coast Road, Danielle beside him in the front seat watching the various lights whirling passed in the darkness. She turns around to check on Simon in the back seat, scrunched at the end, his head dropped down. She thinks he may be crying, but can't tell.

"Hey, wanna steer, big girl?" Sam suddenly asks, his head wobbling, his words still slurry.

Grabbing her arm, he pulls her closer and presses her hands onto the steering wheel, then places his hands over hers. They are sweaty and trembling. She's not happy with this game, but when he is in one of these moods, she knows that it's best not to thwart him and concentrates very hard on keeping the car on the road.

Simon raises his head, his face all ashen, his body jerking left and right by the rough movements.

Exiting at Limerick Beach, Sam takes his hands off hers so Danielle can steer the car up to the front of the house without his help. He goads her on, "Att-agirl!!"

Her hands are sweating now, too, her heart thumping.

As soon as the car comes to a stop, Simon jumps out and stomps into the house.

When Sam and Danielle emerge, Sam throws her over his shoulder like a sack of potatoes. She tries to get away from him, but he is strong. He stinks too, and has that scary look in his eyes. She's had it with him, and wiggles fiercely to try and get away.

He carries her inside, then stands her on her feet. She retreats into the living room while Sam heads straight to the liquor cabinet. Finding it empty, he goes to a bookshelf, takes a bottle of brandy from behind "Tale of Two Cities" and begins fixing a drink.

"Minnie, my beautiful wwwife!" he calls out as she walks in.

Minnie reaches over and pulls the liquor bottle out of his hand.

"You don't need it, Sam. You've had enough."

Sam tugs at the bottle. Danielle's neck sinks into the collar of her red hoodie, like a turtle going into its shell. She flops down on the couch, too scared to pass through and leave the room, and too worried about what will happen next.

Sam's voice has turned hard.

"What, Minnie? So, we're sorta late! Aren't you … over-reacting?"

He tries to put his arm around her, "C'mon, Babe, you used to be more fun."

Minnie lets go of the bottle. She squirms out from his arm, turns and leaves him standing alone. He takes a swig from the bottle and notices Danielle on the couch.

"There's my little race-car driver!"

He staggers across the room and drops onto the couch next to her, flinging his arm over her shoulder, but mis-aiming, he smacks her left ear with his heavy college ring.

It stings and her ear rings, but she holds back the tears.

"Oh, oh, oh, my little wee one. Oh, Dani, so sorry ... so sorry, Babe," Sam mutters, running his fingers through her tangled hair.

Simon stands in the hall doorway. He has on his Scottish plaid pajamas, but the top is mis-buttoned. "Danielle," he says in a scared voice. "I need your help. Can you come ... please?"

Danielle pulls her head away from her father's hand, and jumps up off the couch.

"Sure, Simon. C'mon." she says as she grabs his pajama sleeve on the way out into the hallway. "Thanks for saving me, Si," she adds as they are climbing the stairs.

"Did he hurt you?" Simon asks.

Simon can see by her eyes and the red ear that he did, even though Danielle shakes her head.

"No, no. It's okay. I might have a Hobbit ear to-morrow, that's all ..."

Simon stops before his bedroom door until Danielle waves him to go in. After he does, she goes into her own room. She climbs into bed with her clothes on and tries to think of something else - the skateboard competition coming up, Flopsie's wriggly nose, Nicky - anything but what just happened.

Then she smells Beckett on her blanket, and rolls over to her side, her nose into the blanket. She misses her something terrible.

She has to roll over on her back when the throbbing in her left ear gets worse.

CHAPTER 43

(My job at the Old Age Home is this: I am brought in to various residents, particularly the ones that are especially old or especially sad, and then for half an hour or so this person pets me or speaks to me, or simply watches as I curl up and doze at the foot of their wheelchair or bed. That's it! Easy-peasy! All I have to do is BE ME! Being me seems to make these old people feel better. It's not a bad life. Also, the food is pretty generous! Plus, some people slip me a cracker from their soup plate or a hunk of their cheesecake or a mint from their robe pocket. Perks!

This afternoon I'm curled up in Mr. Maxwell's lap, on top of a blanket that covers the stumps where his legs had been amputated due to an advanced case of diabetes. When he starts snoring, I pine for Danielle, Simon, even that neurotic bird and or dumb rabbit.)

Some miles away, Danielle, Simon and Minnie sit nervously in the waiting room of the Pacific Institute. Minnie's fiddling with her iPhone, checking Facebook. Simon is staring at Danielle's red ear. Danielle is staring into space, her tangled hair in desperate need of washing.

(I'd say her hair has really gotten rather bedraggled. She's starting to look rather doggish, but not in a good way.)

Harry Harding, a beefy guy with a receding hairline who could easily be Sam's older brother, is the counselor at the Institute. He invites them into his office where there's no desk, just chairs around a low table.

As soon as she sits down, Minnie tells Harry, "Now that we're here, I think we're over-reacting."

"To what?" asks Harry.

Simon is rubbing his eyes as if they itch. Danielle examines her shoes.

"This is painful for you, isn't it?" he says to the kids.

Simon's lips begin to tremble. Danielle's face shows nothing, since it's hidden by her messy hair.

"What I mean is," Minnie explains, "perhaps we're over-reacting to … uh … stress at home with Sam, with the kids' dad, my husband."

Determination grips Danielle. She looks directly at her mother.

"Come on, Mom, we're here because of Dad's drinking!"

Defensively, Minnie snaps, "I'm not. I'm here for you kids." Then, looking at Harry, adds, "It's not that bad."

Harry speaks in a friendly but practical tone of voice.

"Listen up, folks. I can help you assess the situation, to determine if a problem exists. That's IF. How does that sound? But first, try to relax."

Minnie takes a deep breath

"I'm going to go through a list of symptoms," he explains, passing out cans of soda to everyone, "and if we determine that a problem exists with Mr. Godot, we can try to figure out how bad it is. For instance, have you noticed any memory problems when he drinks?"

Danielle and Minnie answer at the same moment. Danielle says, "Yes", and Minnie says, "Not recently."

Harry directs his next question to Minnie.

"Have there been times when your husband was drinking that he became aggressive or abusive, either verbally or physically?"

"No. He never would."

Finding it hard to hear someone dump on her dad, Danielle winces.

"Ever see a personality change when he's drinking?"

Tears build in Simon's eyes.

"Simon?" Harry asks.

"Yeah, he got up at a restaurant and danced on the stage like a ... jerk."

"That qualifies. Aggressive needn't mean nasty," Harry explains, "more like, his self-control is lowered."

"What's self-control?" Simon asks.

"Self-control is when you decide what you want to do. Loss of self-control is when you're not completely in charge of yourself."

"Like a monster," Simon replies.

"Sort of, yeah."

Harry turns back to Minnie.

"Have you noticed that he's preoccupied with alcohol?"

Minnie's uncertain. "What do you mean?"

"Does he look forward to a certain time of day? On Saturday morning saying he wishes it were twelve, because at noon he can crack open a beer. Something like that?"

Minnie shakes her head.

"Does he drink alone?"

Minnie shakes her head again. "Only socially, with me or other people ... he -"

Danielle cuts in: "Mom, c'mon! He was alone in front of the TV the other night. It was still on when he fell asleep with his drink in front of him. And it's not the first time!"

Before too long, there's a pile of used tissues in Simon's lap while Danielle slinks lower and lower in her chair.

The questions continue.

"Have you noticed or heard him talk about being generally scared? Not afraid of real things like losing his job or getting hit by a truck, but having a free-floating, indefinable fear?"

Minnie shakes her head.

Simon scratches his head.

Danielle's swollen ear has gotten achy so she pulls her red hood over it.

(Hey! I just thought of something: Danielle and I both now have something more in common: damaged ears!)

CHAPTER 44

At the Limerick Beach football stadium, the scoreboard shows

LIMERICK BEACH – 21, VISITORS – 20.

A night game is nearly finished, almost the last of the season. The Limerick fans are clamoring for a win.

Sam roves up and down the sidelines. His team is near the goal line. He shouts to the wide receiver, "Eight-eight, come here. Left side bootleg."

He claps his hand and smacks Number 88 on the shoulder. Number 88 runs onto the field and the fans cheer.

Sam's so nervous he wishes he had taken a nip of whiskey before the game to steady his nerves. If only they can keep their slim lead! A winning team will make everything right again.

CHAPTER 45

Harry leans back in his chair.

"That's the last question in the third, chronic phase." He sighs, "That's about it."

Simon tries to calculate on his fingers. "Let's see … twenty-nine questions and …"

"There were thirty-one, Si," Danielle interrupts. "And I answered with eight Yeses and two Maybes and mom said five Yeses, one Maybe. YOU were silent!"

"Well, I don't know what most of it means," Simon mutters.

"I'd say he has a pretty low score, huh, kids?" Minnie sighs with relief. "I told you he wasn't …"

Harry shakes his head.

"Any four and he's in the club."

"But … he never really staggers, he never has a hangover."

"And he's never hit us," Simon adds, then remembering Danielle's ear, mumbles, "Well, I mean, like, HIT us …"

Danielle looks up, stares at Harry. "Mr. Harding, my dad acts strange at times. I don't know why. But, I mean, he's usually pretty normal."

"Kids, I know how difficult this is to hear."

Minnie's spine straightens. "May … maybe if I were just a better wife none of this would be happening," she says snatching one of the tissues from Simon's lap and blowing her nose quietly.

"So what do YOU think?" Danielle asks Harry.

"There are enough symptoms to suggest that your dad is in trouble with alcohol, Danielle."

"You mean he's an ..." she can hardly say it, "... alcoholic?"

Minnie stands and walks to the window.

Harry gently suggests, "I think it would be better for you to understand just what is happening to him and then make a determination for yourself as to whether he's an alcoholic."

Seeing Simon's confused looks, Harry pats him on the head.

"Sounds like jargon to me," Minnie snaps acidly.

"Simply, an alcoholic is addicted to alcohol. Being ADDICTED means that the use of alcohol or some other chemical, say pills or even prescription drugs, is causing problems in a major area of that someone's life. If this use continues, there's a good chance he or she will be in need of more and more, whether psychologically or physically."

When Minnie lights a cigarette, the children look at her in shock. "Mom, you weren't going to ever smoke again!" Simon gasps.

Harry goes on, "In which case it means he or she has a life threatening illness." He pauses to let what he's said sink in.

"Can't you just tell us what to do, how to behave? Tell me what I'm doing wrong?" Minnie demands, dropping the cigarette into the soda can, "I mean, you're asking me to be disloyal to my husband."

"Yeah," Danielle adds, "disloyal to my dad who might just have something growing on his brain while you call him all kinds of bad names."

"No, I'm not, Danielle." Harry takes a breath. "Look, you're all here out of caring and concern for your dad. I know you love him. But you have to WANT to understand what's really going on. I'm not pressuring you one way or the other. The motivation has to come from you."

Danielle looks at Simon, then at her mother. "What if we don't tell Dad?"

"There's nothing wrong with keeping your visits here just between us for now, if it will help you feel better," Harry answers. "We have family groups, people like you who get together for a few sessions of films, lectures, discussions."

"Films?" Simon's eyes widen. "Like 'The Hobbit' and stuff?"

Danielle turns to him and crosses her eyes. She notices how her mom is hesitating to make any decision. "MOM!!"

She turns to Danielle, "Only if you insist, Dani. I somehow think we're being over-sensitive. If we all just made an extra effort to be more ... more ..."

"Mom, please. We have to TRY SOMETHING!"

The moods are dark when they pile into her car. Thoughts are colliding—a mix of doubt, fear, confusion and guilt, but also concern, curiosity and a sliver of hope.

On the way home, they stop for ice cream. But, even that doesn't make anything easier.

And Danielle realizes that she is perhaps losing a lot more than her dog.

CHAPTER 46

Danielle and Nicky have taken the Dobermans for a run in the dog park. Nicky's getting more and more attached to these big, feisty not overly-bright dogs. He and Danielle stand at the wrought iron fence, eating licorice rope and watching as the Dobermans cavort with other big dogs.

Nicky asks her, "What do you like most about dogs?"

"I like that they don't carry grudges. What do you like most about dogs?"

He gives a piece of licorice to a Golden Retriever he's been petting that's put its front paws on the fence. The taste registers on its tongue, and it makes a strange face and spits out the black candy.

"I like when I can play with them as rough as I want and they won't get hurt. Also, I like it that they'll protect me from bullies."

(If I were with them instead of being petted by a 104-year-old lady with pink hair, I'd have a word to say about that. I'm smallish, but I'm fast and smart, and am just as much a protector as any old big, stinky dog. Or three nameless Dobermans! And - I LOVE LICORICE!)

The big water bowl inside the gate is kicked over by a Great Dane. Danielle goes into the play area, gets the bowl and carries it over to the water fountain. She fills it, and carries it back inside. As soon as she sets the bowl down several thirsty dogs push her out of the way to get at it, noisily lapping with tongues dipping and dripping.

Quickly, it's empty. Danielle again fills it with water.

Returning to Nicky's side, she realizes he's eaten or fed most of the licorice to various dogs. He looks over to her and brings a finger to her bruised ear.

"So are you gonna tell me what happened to your ear?" he asks.

"Just bumped it," she lies, then to change the subject asks, "Hey, why is a dog's nose in the middle of his face?" as she grabs what remains in the licorice bag.

"Why?" asks Nicky, removing a pear from a plastic bag in his backpack and offering Danielle a bite.

She pushes the pear away.

"I hate pears," she tells him.

Nick begins to nibble on the pear.

"So, why is a dog's nose in the middle of his face?" she repeats.

"Why?"

"Because it is the scenter. Get it?" she points at her nose, "In the center ... the scenter."

"That one ... stinks!" Nicky comments, cracking up at his own joke.

One of the Dobermans bounds over to the fence and snatches Nicky's pear. Now it is Danielle who is cracking up. There are pink streaks cross the sky as one by one the dogs are being led away by their owners. Danielle can't think of any more jokes, and doesn't want Nicky to ask any more serious questions, so she grabs the Dobermans and puts the leashes back around their necks.

They pass through the park gate and turn on to the sidewalk.

"Hey, what do you think Mrs. Harper would say if I asked to take one or two of these guys home," Nicky wonders, "… to kind of try out having dogs for a night?"

Danielle thinks about it while they mount their skateboards. She holds the leash of one of the dogs, and Nicky holds the other two. She knows how much the dogs like Nicky and how much Nicky likes the dogs. Is she crazy to say what she's about to say?

"Sure. Why not take them home for a sleepover?" she blurts out after they've been pulled for half a block.

"I'll break it to Mrs. Harper. I think it'll be okay with her. But if it's not, will you bring them right back to her place?"

Nicky's eyes light up as a thrill runs through him.

"Sure. I'll have them back in a flash if she gets mad," he promises as he flaps the leashes and the two dogs pull him off.

"Yippee!" he yells, wild with happiness.

Danielle's glad she could be the cause of it, but is miffed because it's she who is missing a dog and yet it's Nicky who is getting not one but two!

(There's a saying in People Talk - "A bird in the hand is worth two in a bush." I guess it means that "Two half-witted dogs at hand are better than one bright but missing dog." And though that may be true for Nicky, I'm not so sure about Danielle. At least, it better not be!)

CHAPTER 47

Leaving her skateboard in the back yard, Danielle lets the lone Doberman into Mrs. Harper's kitchen, wondering how she is going to explain the absence of the other two.

She shouts, "Mrs. Harper!"

There's no response, so Danielle ventures into the living room, where Mrs. Harper sits in front of the TV watching the shopping channel. Seeing Danielle, she asks, "Do I know you?"

Danielle points to herself, saying, "Me red Robin Hood, your neighbor."

The Doberman nuzzles Mrs. Harper, who suddenly strikes her forehead with the palm of her hand and leaps up.

"Oh, gosh, it's time to feed you!"

The dog follows her into the kitchen, Danielle follows, too.

"Mrs. Harper, my friend Nicky and I are hoping that you won't mind if …" she starts to explain, then realizes Mrs. Harper can't hear her.

Mrs. Harper has opened a can of dog food and grabs a big spoon. She goes over to where three bowls are set side by side on the floor on a mat.

"I don't know what's wrong with me, Robin Hood. Why do I use three bowls when, even though he's big, one is enough for this guy?"

Danielle stares at her perplexed.

"But, Mrs. Harper, you have …" She starts to set things straight, then shuts up.

Mrs. Harper, meanwhile, picks up two of the bowls and puts them into the sink to wash. She spoons the entire can of food into the one bowl and the dog noisily gobbles it up.

"What were you telling me?" she asks.

"Never mind," Danielle answers, "I gotta go."

"Bye, Robin Hood. Thanks for walking my doggie. You'd better hurry, they say it's going to rain."

Mrs. Harper strokes the dog's neck and ears as it licks the bottom of the bowl. "Oh, if only I could remember your name …"

Danielle mutters to herself as she passes through Mrs. Harper's back yard, "Is EVERY adult around here on another planet?"

CHAPTER 48

Nine people - five adults and four kids - are gathered in the conference room at the Pacific Institute. Danielle, Simon and Minnie are among them. They have been watching a film on a large screen about alcoholism.

Danielle concentrates on the facts and figures, while Simon fidgets with a plastic straw from the slushy Minnie bought him on the way. He notes the absence of elves or dwarves in it and tries to stay awake. Danielle gets a lump in her throat while watching the film. Though she didn't used to be so easily upset, these past months have taken their toll. She turns and looks towards the window. Outside it's raining cats and dogs.

(We dogs never understood why humans say that about a heavy, pounding rain. It is rather insulting, actually. But since it doesn't often rain at all in this area, such a downpour makes everyone jittery – some humans drive too slow in the rain, others drive too fast. We dogs and other animals know to stay clear of the roads on days like this.)

Back at the high school, Sam stands at a blackboard outlining a football play. His team sits in the classroom in front of him, making notes on the play while Sam is explaining. As he talks, he glances out the window at the heavy rain that's streaking the glass. His stomach is filled with butterflies: if it doesn't stop raining soon, the game will get called.

CHAPTER 49

By the following Saturday, the days of rain have ended and Sam's game has gone on as scheduled and the end of football season is getting close. The air is fresh, the sky bright blue again.

(Since the cat-and-dog-rain has finally stopped, I'm being taken out for walks so I can add my pee to all the lawns around the old age home. I haven't had this much fun since Danielle and Nicky set me free on the beach one day and let me catch the Frisbee they were throwing back and forth! Oh, darn! ... now I'm thinking about Danielle again!)

Danielle is across town with Simon and their mom and the same group gathered at the Pacific Institute's conference room. There are yellow pads in front of each person and, again, some are taking notes.

On the blackboard is written:

LIVER AILMENTS
NERVE DISORDERS – often in feet or hands
PSYCHOSIS – mental crack up

Danielle writes down every word, even if she doesn't get its total meaning. "What IS the liver for again?" she wonders, trying to remember what she learned in biology class. Still, she knows it is important, and makes a mental note to Google all the terms on the blackboard when she gets home.

Harry adds:

ORGANIC BRAIN SYNDROME

to the list, explaining, "In a nutshell, what all this means is that drinking hurts the brain. That's the bad news. The drinker's memory begins to go, he or she has trouble concentrating and makes bad decisions."

He turns from the board to face the group, continuing, "This gets worse the longer the drinking goes on."

Danielle adds the new descriptions to her list. She wants to get it all right.

"But, if the alcohol abuse stops then the person's memory, concentration and judgment can improve a lot as the brain bounces back over months or years of recovery. That's the good news."

Harry speaks directly to a teenage girl in the group who has a row of at least ten silver piercings along her right ear. Danielle wonders why anybody would do that to a body part! Besides, that sort of thing went out of fashion long ago.

"Hence, Carol, your mother putting the butter in the washing machine and the dirty socks in the refrigerator."

Everyone laughs. He turns toward to the elderly gentleman in the group.

"Or your son forgetting where he parked the car, Pedro."

Harry's eyes scan the whole group.

"The alcoholic is usually the last one to realize what his trouble is. He blames everything else but alcohol. The key word is 'denial'." He writes the word DENIAL on the board in very large letters.

Danielle writes the word in her notebook and underlines it. At least that one she knows!

Simon, though, does not, and mutters to Danielle, "Why is the key word The Nile? It's a river, no?"

She bops him on the head with her notepad and turns back to Harry.

He puts down the chalk. "And believe me, folks, in your alcoholic's heart of hearts, he doesn't think drinking is his problem. He does not see alcohol as a powerful mind-drug, and, sadly, neither does our society. Forgive me if I sound preachy, but ours is a society where over forty percent of the people in our prisons are there because of an alcohol or drug-related crime; a society whose industry suffers tens of billions of dollars of lost-time yearly because of alcohol and drug abuse; where over thirty thousand people are killed on our highways as a result of drinking drivers, and two and one half million are maimed. It's a scourge."

He pauses and concludes, "Ours is a society where one in ten drinkers becomes alcoholic."

While listening, Minnie crosses and uncrossed her legs. Simon's eyelids are drooping but Danielle is tuned in since just maybe this is the answer to her dad's problem.

But she wishes she knew what 'scourge' means.

(And me, I'm wondering - if Sam gets fixed, maybe he will make an effort to find me and I can come back home! I miss

Danielle's cuddles, and riding with her on her skateboard, and sleeping under her covers instead of alone in the broom closet at this place. And, I don't like it at all that's she's getting on so well with that ditsy Doberman next door. Oh, and scourge is a noun - 'a thing that causes great trouble or suffering'.)

CHAPTER 50

The following week the team bus is speeding down the freeway toward the second to last game of the season. The players are sprawled across the seats. Holding on to the overhead rack, Sam stands at the front of the bus, explaining, "We're using the three-four defense because number thirty-two is such a good RB."

He takes a list out of his pocket, refers to it. "Their QB is a lousy thrower so we don't have to worry about the pass."

(And I thought watching TV with the Godot's was boring! How did Sam memorize all this sporty-lingo stuff? Pardon me if I go off to take a nap or watch a fly crawl across the window ...)

The bus suddenly swerves as the highway twists to the right causing Sam to lose his balance and nearly fall over.

"Hey, Coach, you all right?" a player close to him asks.

Sam has regained his balance but his face has gotten all sweaty and his hands are clammy. "Yeah, yeah, I'm fine. Thanks. Just a little dehydrated."

The player jumps up to help him. "It wasn't THAT violent a turn, Mr. Godot. Sure you're okay?"

Sam shoos him away and takes a large gulp from his bottle of mineral water. The liquid inside is a little bit cloudy to be just water.

CHAPTER 51

Danielle and Nicky sit at their usual table in the back corner of the lunchroom at school. On each tray - a burrito and a small carton of milk.

"So? SO? How's it going? Tell me!" Danielle demands.

"There isn't enough room on my bed for both dogs," Nicky explains after a sip of milk. "Or, if there is, there's no room for me, so I gave them the bed and now I sleep in the teepee."

Danielle's eyes moisten.

"What? What'd I say?" Nicky asks.

"Nothing. It's just ... well, it makes me homesick for Beckett. It's been so darn long now, I'm beginning to wonder if I'll ever see her again." Danielle picks up the burrito. Melted cheese oozes from a fold in the tortilla.

Nicky is quiet, pulling the drippy cheese from his. He asks, "Like … are you sure Mrs. Harper said I could keep them?"

"Wouldn't I tell you if there was a problem? Even one Doberman is almost too much for Mrs. Harper. She's really old. Trust me, Nicky, you're doing her a favor. "

Nicky narrows his eyes. Something's not right, but he doesn't know what. "Hey, did you know that losing your head in an emergency is a no-brainer," Nicky jokes, expecting she'll crack a smile. Which she doesn't.

"C'mon, any new elephant jokes?" he asks, a bit of cheese stuck to his upper lip.

"No. I've run out," Danielle replies. "There's one about an elephant in the living room … but it doesn't have a punch line."

Nicky gives up trying to cheer her up.

Danielle knows that Nick is trying to be a pal. She appreciates his efforts but it only makes her feel guilty about not telling him she's been going to the Institute and that she hasn't told Mrs. Harper about giving him the dogs. She's never kept secrets from him before, and it doesn't feel very good.

"Hey, you can come over anytime for a sleepover. Mom and Dad said so," Nicky reminds her, breaking a long silence. "I have all three 'Lord of the Rings' on Blu-ray!" he adds.

"Cool," Danielle mutters after swallowing a bite of warm burrito.

"AND − I want you to help me come up with names for the Dobermans. It's hard to train them without names, and they -" remembering that talking of dogs is what was upsetting her, he drops it.

"Anyhow, maybe this weekend, huh?"

"Yeah, maybe."

She looks at Nicky as he finishes his burrito. He's a great pal. Maybe soon she'll be ready to tell him everything. Maybe.

CHAPTER 52

At the Institute, the same group has gathered. Harry explains that today they will do something called "role-playing" as he moves two empty chairs to the front of the room and sets them down facing each other. The remaining chairs form a loose circle.

Harry calls out, "Okay, let's try this out. Would Carol and Nelly Stein take these chairs?"

Carol and her identical twin sister Nelly get up and sit in the chairs face-to-face.

"Okay. Carol, you'll play your mother, and Nelly, you'll be yourself, the daughter."

"Now, who remembers the 'DON'TS'?" he asks the group.

Danielle raises her hand, and also Pedro, who hasn't shaved the gray stubble off his chin but has a new hearing aid in one ear.

"Danielle."

"Don't dump or hide alcohol. Don't punish, bribe or threaten the alcoholic into quitting. The desire to quit must come from him, or her!"

Minnie tilts her head and grins at her daughter. Simon sticks out his tongue at her and mumbles, "Know it all!"

"Good, Danielle," Harry nods. "And Pedro?"

"Don't argue with him or her when they're drunk."

Pedro looks at his wife and continues, "Don't cover up for him. Don't take responsibility for him or her."

Pedro's wife, Marina, rolls her eyes. "I don't care what you say," she explains to the group. "He's my son, and if he asks me to call his boss and say he's sick, I'll do it. I'll cover for him. What's the big deal?"

"You're not helping him when you shield him from the consequences of his drinking." Harry adds, "You are -"

Danielle finishes his sentence, "- reinforcing his denial, helping him kill himself."

Marina throws up her hands. "So I'm guilty one way or the other. Doomed if I do, doomed if I don't."

"That's why people closest to the alcoholic get nutty, too," Harry explains, "… why they need help, too."

He looks at the twins.

"So, Carol, you'll be your mother and Nelly, you be yourself."

"You said that already," Simon reminds him.

"So I did, Simon. Sorry. Now," back to the girls, "What shall the setting be? Use a real incident."

"Well, there was this time Mom busted up my sweet sixteen party by getting drunk," Carol suggests. "Oh, here's the worst part, she was wearing only a bra and ..." She closes her eyes, "... a thong."

"How did you feel?" Harry asks her.

"Ashamed. Grossed out."

Playing the mom, Nelly messes up her hair, pulls her sweater off one shoulder and opens another button. The group titters.

"And," Carol adds, "she flirted with my boyfriend!"

Simon mumbles, "Ew!" while scrunching up his face.

Danielle elbows him lightly in the side.

"Oww," he mutters.

(Ooowwww. Ooowwww. I've taken up howling to release my Inner Wolf, hoping it calms down my anxiousness at A)being Danielle-less, and B)adjusting to my new job ... Ooooowwww ...)

Meanwhile, across town, Sam is shouting, "Oww! Wow, wow wow!!"

The scoreboard at the high school stadium shows that his team has actually won! There is wild pandemonium among the crowd, and the football players are screaming and jumping all over each other landing in a big pile.

One player breaks from the pile and leaps into Sam's arms, mussing up his wavy hair. The other players hoist Sam up on their shoulders and carry him around the field.

Sam is overjoyed. Finally, just as the football season is coming to an end, everything is okay! They're not champions. But they're not at the bottom of the league either. If they can hold their own in the final game next week, there'll be a good reason to celebrate.

CHAPTER 53

Danielle has decided to sleep over at Nicky's. It's Friday night, so there's no school the next day. Plus she's tired of all this serious talk about livers and disorders and denial and just wants to be silly. She's got on her purple pajamas and Nicky his white and blue striped ones, his initial N on the top pocket. He sits on the floor leaning against the bed that Danielle is on, the two Dobermans curled up on either side of her. Her hands reach over and pet their bellies. Nicky has chosen names, he tells her. One is now called Nameless, and the other is No-Name.

She stops rubbing their bellies, thinking about whether or not she likes those names. She isn't sure. "Toy Story 3" has been playing on the small flat screen TV, but they're not paying much attention to it.

"Hey, I've got one for you about dogs," Nicky brags.

"Shoot."

"Why does your dog keep turning around in circles?"

"Why?"

"He's a watch dog and he's winding himself."

Nicky waits for Danielle to respond. But, instead of laughing or smiling, her lip curls.

"Beckett sometimes turned round and round in circles," Danielle remembers mournfully. Then adds, "Nicky, can we stick with elephants, please?"

"Or, what about … SKATEBOARDS!?" he asks, pulling one out from under his bed. It is brand new, unscratched, a label still stuck on the surface.

Danielle sits up so abruptly that one of the dogs leaps off the bed. "Wow, Nick! That's the one you showed me in the catalogue, right? Cool!"

"Yep, that's the one."

Danielle slumps down onto the floor next to him, sliding her fingers across the new skateboard and around the bright red wheels, her eyes wide and sparkling.

"Happy birthday," Nicky sings, rolling it towards her.

"You're joking. You know perfectly well it's not my birthday."

"Yeah, but we were away at the cabin for your last one, so Mom said I should order you one when I was getting mine," Nicky explains, sliding his hand under the bed and rolling out a second one that has day-glow green wheels.

"And anyway, yours is all battered and the wheels are worn," he adds.

Danielle feels like giving Nicky a hug. But instead shouts, "Tomorrow! Just you wait! With this thing I'll whiz right past you!"

The Dobermans leap up and scurry out the door. Someone has whistled for them to come get their dinner.

(Yes! I say. YES! Get rid of those overgrown nit-wits! It is I who should be with Danielle and Nicky and the new skateboards and the bag of chips nearby! It is I who should be invited to the slumber party, getting my belly rubbed, watching "Toy Story 3" for the fifth time, falling sleeping under the quilt with Danielle.)

CHAPTER 54

Harry stands at the blackboard. The chairs are lined up classroom style. The word

INTERVENTION

is written on the board, and Danielle notes it in her book.

"Victims of alcoholism do not usually submit to treatment because of a sudden insight," Harry lectures. "Nor do they have to hit the proverbial 'bottom'. A bottom can be induced through some form of in-ter-ven-tion - it's a way of motivating an alcoholic into treatment."

Harry notices that the Godot kids are not sure what he's talking about. He points to the Stein twins.

"The Steins here are planning an intervention on their mother. An intervention is when meaningful people confront the alcoholic with factual data about their drinking in a non-judgmental way."

Minnie says, "But 'intervention' sounds so aggressive, so confrontational."

Harry nods his head in agreement.

"You're right. Perhaps it's the wrong word. It does sort of conjure an attack. Intervention is more of a presentation of facts and feelings offered with love and concern ... you're trying to get them to SEE the reality of what they're doing."

"My son would kill me if I did such a thing," Marina says.

Minnie goes even further, "There's no way I'd do that."

"So, what else can we do to make him stop?" Danielle asks Harry.

"You can't MAKE him stop. You can't change him, Danielle."

"Then what good is all this?"

"The only one you can change is yourself."

Danielle slaps her notebook shut. "Excuse me, but I'M not the one with the problem. Why should I have to change, it's my dad who has the problem?!"

"A family is like a mobile hanging from the ceiling," Harry explains. "If YOU change the balance will shift, and it might make him WANT to change too."

"But Sam isn't like Mrs. Stein," Minnie tells Harry and the group, "He doesn't put lampshades on his head at parties or walk around in a thong. He doesn't disappear for days at a time. Mrs. Stein sounds like she'll be put away or dead if someone doesn't do something about her. If Sam's got it at all - which I'm still not convinced - he's only got a touch. Barely."

Harry looks right at Minnie. "There's no such thing as being 'just a touch' pregnant, is there? Unfortunately alcoholism is a progressive, permanent and fatal illness."

Abruptly Simon stands up and recites: "There once was a lady from Spain, Who got sick while riding a train. Not once but a-gain, and a-gain and a-gain. And a-gain and a-gain and a-gain."

The group half-heartedly snickers, then seriousness takes over again.

"God, this isn't going to be easy," Danielle mutters to herself. "I wish it were a year from now and I've won the Skateboarding Championship, and Dad's just drinking lemonade, and Beckett is back home on my bed chewing on a bone or even my sneakers."

(Me too! Me too!)

CHAPTER 55

After the session at the Institute, Simon, Danielle and Minnie go to the pier for a stroll and an ice cream cone and to meet Sam after his very last football game has finished. There's a sign at the front of the pier in the shape of a whale that reads:

SORRY FOLKS, NO DOGS, HORSES, FIRE, OR ALCOHOL

(This sign, quite frankly, offends me as a dog. I mean, putting me, a cute furry little sweet thing, on the same list as fire and alcohol! Please! Who writes these signs?)

Danielle notices this insult to dogs and thinks how she could never bring Beckett to the pier for a walk, to smell the smells, maybe ride on the bumper cars or the Ferris wheel, and she gets even sadder than the thing about her dad has made her.

They are all a bit nervous. They don't want Sam to be upset if his team has lost. And ... they hope he won't be too curious about where they've just been. As they stroll, Simon looks over the side at the surfers in wetsuits lying flat out on their boards, and taps at Danielle to look down, too. She does and wishes she were one of them in a cool, black wetsuit.

"Maybe in Forest Green," she mutters to herself. "Why must I have a black one just because everybody else does?"

Moving on, they pass a few fishermen near the bait and tackle shop.

"How many?" Danielle asks one of the fishermen.

"Nothin' yet, Honey."

Minnie recognizes the little girl there fishing with her father. "Hi, Eva."

"Oh, hi, Mrs. Godot." The girl tells her father, "That's my dancing school teacher."

The father smiles at Minnie.

Danielle feels like they own the pier, that it belongs to them, since they've walked up and down it all their lives. It never changes. After another lick of ice cream she notices a young couple walking toward them with a dog. The scruffy dog has pointy ears just like Beckett.

"Beckett!!" Danielle yells.

"Where? You see Beckett?" Simon shouts, as his sister points at the dog that's not more than ten yards away.

Danielle begins to run towards it, but before she's gone five steps she stops. She's drenched with disappointment because, though the dog's almost as cute as her dog (but not quite), it's got two complete ears, not one and a half. Also, it's a male. Also, it's cross-eyed.

She pounds Simon on the shoulder with her fist. Biting his lip, Simon doesn't stop her.

"I'm sorry, Dani." Minnie ruffles the top of her head.

"I'm sorry, too."

(I'm not sorry at all. I'm thrilled that Danielle still misses me so much, that wherever she goes, whatever she is doing, she is on the look-out for me. I sure wish I were with her right now because Danielle used to give me the last pointy bit of her ice cream cone, always making sure there was a little left in it for me. Especially cookie dough flavor – she knew I liked that best.)

As the couple with the dog-that's-not-Beckett passes, Simon snottily tells them, "No dogs on the pier, folks. Maybe you didn't see the sign."

The couple give Simon a dirty look.

(I'd give him a dirty look, too! I mean, they used to always take ME to places I wasn't allowed - but never the pier! Some rules are just silly.)

At the end of the pier they stand together looking out at the horizon far away for a few moments. until Minnie begins to speak.

"So back to our conversation in the car," she says. "Here's the plan: I don't see any need for us to keep going there. We don't say anything about the Institute to Dad. I think we've learned a lot but that's enough of that. We can handle this by ourselves. Agreed?"

Both kids nod.

"Are you still going to drink, Mom?" asks Danielle.

Before she can answer they hear Sam's booming voice shouting, "Danielle! Simon! Minnie! We won! We won!!! WE WON!!!"

They turn to see Sam running along the pier - sprinting - toward them, throwing a football up into the air and catching it as he runs.

Danielle responds first and runs to greet him.

"Bueno, Papa! Mucho Bueno!"

Reaching him she leaps up, clinging onto his shoulders like she used to all the time.

"Oh, Dani, it was so great! We actually won!"

"I'm so happy for you, Dad," she says hugging him more than she has in a long, long time.

"And I'm sorry for the way I've been behaving … you know. I feel much better now," Sam beams at her. "Everything's okay now … It's okay."

Simon and Minnie hug him as well. With his arms around all three, he offers them a meal at the restaurant on the end of the pier to celebrate.

(A restaurant! Now I REALLY wish I were there! They don't call them doggy bags for nothing!)

PART THREE

FACING UP TO THE ELEPHANT

CHAPTER 56

The winter holidays have come and gone. Christmas and New Year's were better than expected, with Sam drinking only apple cider or ginger ale and an occasional beer at all the festivities. After celebrating the end of football season and cracking a rib on the stairway, he had decided to cut back his drinking almost to nothing. In solidarity, Minnie also did, and Danielle and Simon wonder if that's the end of that. They enjoyed nearly everything about the holidays, too. Well, most everything. Their grandma arrived from Kalamazoo and, as always, made them eat her home-made scrapple every morning (corn meal with pork scraps) and meatloaf for dinner.

Danielle almost swore off meatloaf for life!

(Darn! I would have been in dog heaven since I'm still at the old age home, and my "Christmas meal" was an extra handful of kibble. Cheap kibble. Stale kibble. Just the thought of fried pig parts makes me spin in circles and drool.)

But now it's February, the days are getting longer. And yesterday, out of the blue, Sam increased his drinking again. Just like that. Nothing good or bad had happened. It was just an ordinary day. He simply came home from work that February afternoon and snapped open a beer can. Danielle and Simon heard the snap and cringed. Then, soon enough, came more snaps, and Danielle got up and left the house and skated to Nicky's.

It's the time of year when whales migrate from Mexico to Alaska, passing near to where they live, sometimes close enough to see. Often Danielle and Nicky skate to the Coast Road in hopes of seeing the majestic creatures passing – great thrusts of water whooshing up when they surface to breathe.

"I wish I were a whale," Danielle remarks when, after waiting around for a very long time, they actually spy a pod of six or seven whales rising one by one to the surface.

"Really? A whale? Well, why?" Nicky asks, lowering his binoculars down from his eyes.

"To get the heck out of here." she replies.

"Well, I don't know if I'd like being in the water all that time. Always swimming, no rest, just eating small fish and plankton. Gross! And, I mean, where do whales sleep? And besides …" he adds, "when's the last time you saw a whale on a skateboard, huh?"

He pokes her ribs and gets a smile from her.

"Yeah, you're right," she sighs. "And anyway, you know how my skin gets like a prune if I stay in the water too long."

They stash the binoculars in Nicky's backpack and pull out granola bars to munch on during the ride home.

That evening Danielle's on the computer in the study looking up ancient Egypt for a school report. Every so often she switches onto a website about whales, trying to find out how they sleep.

And with one ear she's listening for any noises from downstairs, like more snaps.

CHAPTER 57

Danielle recently started doing her school reports in Sam's office room on the computer. Tonight she's supposed to learn about Catherine the Great of Russia. At her side is a bowl of popcorn, still warm, which she munches while examining diagrams on how the Great Pyramids were constructed instead, promising herself she'll get to Catherine the Great real soon.

(Hmm. Curious. At the shelter I spent so long in, there was a small yapping dog named Catherine, another, larger, named Great, and a long sleek grey dog named Russia. I cannot verify, though, that there was one named either The or Of.)

Sam walks in and sits at his desk across the room, where he'd been working on his taxes. On a shelf above him are several plaques and trophies -

CAPTAIN - UCLA FOOTBALL TEAM 1996

FIRST PLACE L.A. MARATHON 2002

Cancelled checks, receipts, tax forms, a calculator, are spread on the desk. There's a squat bottle of Napoleon Brandy and a half-filled glass beside the calculator. He looks perplexed, scratches his head, doodles a bit, takes a sip from the glass, then gets up and looks out of the window.

When Minnie comes in to check on them both he asks her, "Know where I can find the receipts for my car repairs?"

Minnie shakes her head and roams around the room.

"You seem a little distracted, something on your mind, Hon?" he asks.

"Sam ... I -"

Sensing a serious discussing coming on, he cuts in.

"Let's talk later, Sweetheart. If we get into one of our talks, I'll never finish. Plus ... I'm a little hung-over from last night's post-game wake. Why can't my new basketball team at least tie a game?"

Danielle rolls her eyes. "Maybe if you were sober more often. Duh!" she mutters to herself.

"But Sam ..." Minnie tries again, tearing up.

"Okay, okay. Fine. Let's talk."

Danielle picks up the bowl of popcorn and darts out of the room. She's had enough of their little dramas night after night.

Sam wipes Minnie's tears with a tissue. "Have a little brandy, Hon, then tell me what's wrong."

"That's just it. Why must you drink brandy while you work? Can't you just have a cup of coffee?"

"I don't have to drink brandy," he answers, attempting a joke. "I can drink scotch."

She doesn't laugh, but instead bursts out. "Sam, c'mon. PLEASE, listen!"

Sam is surprised that she's raised her voice, and sits down.

Minnie sits in the chair Danielle has vacated. "Why must you drink at all? You cut way back and I was so pleased. Now it's starting all over again! Sam, I'm afraid it will hurt you."

"Me? I'm six two. I'm a big guy. It'd take a lot of booze to hurt me. Besides, it has never affected me, you know that."

"You're not as young as you used to be. Can't you just give it up for a while, clean out the system? I'll do it with you."

"Honey, you forget something. I like a sip or two. It gets my spirit up. I don't feel uptight when I drink."

"But you're drinking almost every night again."

This conversation is starting to annoy Sam. "You know damn well I can take it or leave it alone. C'mon!"

"Can you?"

Feeling pinned down, Sam pushes back. "Yes. I proved it to you guys. And you - YOU'RE so good? Nagging Simon all the time." He mimics her: "'Your bike's in the way of my car. Your shirt's dirty!' Do you know what it does to a kid to get nagged and belittled all the time?"

He's taken the focus away from himself. She rises to the bait and gets defensive.

"How can you say 'all' the time?"

"You're on his back. You're on my back. Danielle's become a little introvert with hair like a jungle animal. And you? You're turning into a kill-joy."

"I? I'm the one who's doing everything around here. Who was supposed to fix the dripping faucet in the kitchen?"

She stands up and kicks the desk. "You don't let me talk to you. And when you do, you don't hear me."

She slams the door behind her. He speaks to the closed door in a patronizing voice, "So talk!"

Upstairs, Danielle has gathered Flopsie and Pickle beside the bowl of popcorn on her bed. She's feeding popcorn to herself with one hand while Flopsie and even Pickle smell and pick at the kernels she gives them. Her heart is hammering. When she hears the sound of the downstairs door slamming, she gets up and shuts the door to her own room. Purposely slamming it hard.

"I guess that's what they mean by an elephant in the living room," she comments to her pets.

(Minus me, of course. At that very moment I am NOT eating popcorn, NOT growling at that bird-brained parakeet, NOT comforting Danielle. I'm in the lap of an old lady watching "101 Dalmatians," a film about ridiculous-looking dogs with spots!

And what's all this talk about elephants, when there are none in sight?)

167

CHAPTER 58

It's a few nights later, and there have been no further arguments. Everyone is in bed except Sam, who is back from a long walk. He stands alone on the porch, glass in hand, admiring the town twinkling below.

He wanders into the kitchen, takes a half-finished bottle of wine from the refrigerator and pours himself a glassful. He turns on the radio, fiddles with the dial until he finds some music from the nineties.

"Yeah!" he says, moving his body to the beat. He turns the handle of the perpetually dripping faucet, trying to fix it. As much as he tries with all his strength, the drip continues. Drip, drip.

He turns the radio volume louder.

Pickle blinks, wishes someone, anyone, would talk with him a little. He's been alone all evening. It's good he's a Buddhist with a lot of patience to begin with.

Sam opens the silverware drawer, and once again there are sharp knives taped-up with duct tape.

Pickle squawks.

Sam removes the taped knives and sets them on the counter. Then one by one he peels the tape revealing steak knives, butcher knives and small paring knives. He unravels them all and puts them back in the drawer. He crumples the tape and throws it into the garbage can.

Drink in hand, he wanders upstairs to Simon's bedroom, and looks in the doorway. Simon's fast asleep, a leg hanging out from under the quilt. Sam sits on the edge of the bed and smoothes Simon's nutmeg-brown hair with the palm of his hand. It's Simon's night with Flopsie, who is asleep in her cage that's on the floor next to the bed. Sam accidentally kicks it, and Flopsie scampers to the farthest corner, her nose twitching double-time.

He moves down the hall and enters Danielle's room. Her bed is cluttered with library books on Catherine the Great, and her new skateboard rests up-side down on the floor. He has trouble finding her face among overgrown hair, and when he does he leans down and lays his cheek against her cheek. He doesn't realize that she's only pretending to be asleep. She's sort of happy to have her father cuddling her, but disgusted by the rancid smell of liquor on his breath.

Finally Sam gets up. As he leaves the room he notices the photo of Beckett that's pinned to the wall beside the door. Seeing Beckett's funny face with one and a half ears makes him wince. He is half out the door when he reaches back in and rips it off the wall.

(No, no! Not that one! That's one of Dani's favorites! Oh boy, is she going to be pissed off!)

In the master bedroom, Minnie is asleep, her head hidden under one of the pillows and her hand thrown back against another. Sam picks up the hand with the glinting wedding ring, holds it, then lets it fall onto the blanket.

He walks back downstairs, has a sip or two of wine right out of the bottle, then picks up the phone and dials a number. A voicemail on the end of the line kicks in: "Surf Travel: Unravel with travel. Max Katz speaking. I'm not at my desk right now, so please leave your name, number and a brief message after the tone and I'll call you back. Wait for the tone, travelers."

What sounds like a ship's whistle follows.

"Hi, pal. It's Sam Godot. Hold onto your tattoos. Finally I'm clear. I want to surprise my family and take my sabbatical. We ALL need to get away. I'm giving the go ahead - please book the tickets we discussed."

He puts down the phone and pours a full glass of wine. He attempts a Greek dance, balancing the glass of wine on his head. Right away it topples, the glass shattering and wine splashing everywhere.

Exhausted and dizzy, he stumbles into the living room, falls onto the couch. He sings along with the latest song playing on the radio then, abruptly, begins to snore.

CHAPTER 59

The next morning Danielle gathers her schoolbooks and shoves them into her backpack. Her eyes stop at the photo of Beckett torn in half and lying on the floor. It was taken on Halloween a year ago, when she and Simon had tied scarves all over their dog, dressing her up as a Gypsy, and is one of her favorites of Beckett.

(See! I told you. And it's one of my favorites of me, too. Although I look rather Bohemian, at least the scarves are covering my bad ear! Being away from Dani so long now I'd let her dress me in dirty rags, or even, her polka dot bikini, if I could just be back at her side.)

She tapes the pieces of the photo back together with Scotch tape, then grabs her pen and notebook and zips the pack closed. Turning to leave, she hears her father calling her mother's name. Then her name. His voice is frantic.

"Minnie? Danielle? Simon? Someone!"

Minnie and Danielle reach the bathroom door at the same time. Sam is kneeling beside the bathtub wearing his big white bathrobe and holding the bathtub stopper in his hand. There's a look of fear on his face and he has broken out in a sweat.

Minnie drops down beside him on the floor. Danielle pauses at the doorway, Simon's head peeking from behind her, reaching for Danielle's hand.

"What? What is it, Sam?" Minnie asks.

"Would you do me a favor, Hon?"

"Sure. Tell me."

"Would you put the stopper in the hole and turn on the bath water for me, please."

Minnie looks at him strangely.

"It sounds silly, but I'm afraid of what might come up out of the drain. I can't look down into it. I can't." He holds the stopper out to her and looks away as she places it over the drain.

"And ... and phone school for me, tell them I've got a bug and won't make it in. I'm really feeling under the weather. Please, be my best friend."

Danielle shudders as she turns away - she doesn't want to see her hero like this.

Simon has put his face against her back, he's frightened.

"C'mon, Si, school," Danielle reminds him, pulling him along by the hand. "It's just Dad acting super-weird again."

CHAPTER 60

Minnie sits across from Harry, leaning forward.

"When I saw him beside the tub so scared, it rang a bell." Her voice is low, as if the truth is stuck in her throat.

"I could see real fear in his eyes as he looked away from the drain. I knew his fear was indefinable, just like you explained in your lecture."

"You've got it, Minnie," Harry answers sympathetically.

"Did you go through this sort of thing, too?" she asks.

Harry nods. "I remember when I was drinking I was afraid I'd drown in my own bed. I couldn't go to the bank, to the supermarket. Stupid as it sounds, I used to think I heard my dirty laundry singing."

Minnie fiddles with the wedding ring on her finger.

"But that was later. Almost at the end," he adds.

"I'm scared. I'm really scared for the kids … for all of us. This illness is poisoning our family." She adds, "Oh, thank you for seeing me. I know we stopped coming here abruptly, but …"

"I understand. You're always welcome back here."

"Why did you drink, Harry? I mean, it ruined your life. It's ruining ours."

"Baudelaire, the French poet, summed up what it's like to be an alcoholic in an apt way. He wrote, 'Only when we drink poison are we well.' It's true. Well, when we drink poison we THINK we are well, though actually it's just the opposite. I remember the first time I drank, at a Christmas party. There was a motley tree with maybe twenty lights. After I'd had my first drink … it looked like there were three thousand shining lights on the tree."

Minnie listens.

"When the music was slow, I danced fast. It was the best night of my life. It made me feel full, like something that had been missing all my life, a hole inside, had gotten filled up. Later, of course, I puked my guts out in the bushes."

The whiny sound of a siren can be heard from outside.

"Alcohol means something to an alcoholic that no one but an alcoholic can understand."

"Why did it take me so long to see it? I'm the closest to him?" Minnie ponders, almost to herself.

"That's what's so tricky about this sickness. The closer you are, often, the harder it is to see. Sometimes the people around are in denial, too, just like the drinker. And Sam's a high bottom at this point."

"High bottom?"

"I mean, he hasn't really fallen very far down. In general, his life is still intact. For now."

Her eyes lock with Harry's eyes. "I want to do an intervention on Sam."

Harry nods and asks, "Who else is concerned?"

"We've all been fooled. Except Danielle. She was trying to tell us in her own way, but we didn't listen."

"Where is she in relation to Sam?"

"Withdrawn from both of us, especially Sam, even though he's always been a kind of hero to her ... and despite having lost her favorite pet."

"Do you think she'd be willing to participate?"

"I'm sure she will. She's had more guts than any of us even though she's suffering with this. As is Simon in his own way."

"Kids often get that something's really wrong before we adults do. First thing, why don't you and the kids talk to a few people who are meaningful to Sam, see who might be willing to participate in an intervention?"

After a short pause he adds, "You never know what sort of conspiracy of silence has been going on."

"Conspiracy of silence?"

"People around you who know something is wrong but don't say anything. You know, the elephant in the living room."

"That's funny. Danielle used that saying a while ago as well. I guess we don't see what we don't WANT to see."

"That's it, Minnie. Listen, you and the kids should talk to those nearest you. Then I'll set up a meeting for us all and you'll begin to put together your lists of non-judgmental data on Sam's drinking. We can see where we stand."

A frightened look crosses Minnie's face as she twists at her ring. "Do marriages break up over this sort of thing?"

"Sometimes. I won't kid you, Minnie."

"He's not a villain, you know. He's a fabulous guy."

"The villain is alcohol, not Sam. We're trying to break through his delusions, not have a witch hunt."

"I'm frightened, Harry. If only things were like they were before Beckett was lost."

(FINALLY, my name has been mentioned! Even though I've been away from them so long now, I still feel like I'm a of the family. If I were there - which I am not, since I'm sitting

on the fuzzy pink slippers of an old woman who's staring out the window at roses - I would be there for the intervention. Absolutely. Problem is, nobody listens to the dog's version of events. Nobody asks us what we pets think. And believe me, we've seen it all.)

CHAPTER 61

Danielle dismounts from her skateboard at Limerick Beach Unified High School. It's the end of the day and students and teachers are criss-crossing everywhere on their way home. She looks this way and that, nibbling on her thumbnail. Finally she spots her father's friend and colleague, Rex Cunningham. He sees her at the same moment. "Hey, Danielle," he calls out in a friendly way.

"I need to speak with you. Can we walk down to the beach?"

"Sure."

With her skateboard under one arm, they walk the few blocks to the beach. Reaching it, Rex stops for a moment to roll up his trouser legs. They both take off their shoes and hold them in their hands as they walk through the soft sand toward the rolling surf. While they walk, Danielle intently explains the situation. Rex stares down at the sand and listens.

By the time they reach the hard sand at the water's edge, Danielle has finished.

"Sam … an alcoholic like the guys that hang out in the bus station? No way," are Rex's first words.

"That's what we thought at first," Danielle replies. "It's nutty."

"Mr. Cunningham, please. We need you on this. We wouldn't ask if Dad didn't need help."

"I can't quite swallow it, Danielle. I've seen him a little tipsy sometimes but have only seen him really drunk once. Once. That was when we won the state championship and we all got sloshed over that. Are you sure you're dealing with reputable people at this institute place? There are fanatics in these areas you know. Sam's just a red-blooded, two-fisted drinker. Nothing wrong with that."

"Will you just think about it? At least read this literature," Danielle begs in a small voice.

Rex nods and Danielle hands him a large envelope.

"Look, I gotta get home, Hon," Rex says after taking the envelope. "I will think about what you said."

After he has gone, Danielle walks towards the ocean and puts her bare feet in the coolness. She likes the feel of the water rushing in, rushing out, with each wave. Impulsively she tosses her shoes and skateboard onto the dry sand, and moves deeper, bending and scooping up some of the foamy water. She wets her face and hair. The water is cold and makes her feel more awake. She splashes her face again and again, the salty ocean washing away the tears that are blurring her vision.

A spotted Dalmatian scampers across the sand and into the surf alongside its owners, causing more tears to fall.

(For the record, that wouldn't be me. No way! Whenever Danielle or the Godot family took me to the beach, I'd dig big holes, chase seagulls, catch flying balls or Frisbees, even take their splashes or the water dumped over me from their sand-castle buckets, but no way would you ever find ME roaming into the ocean! I'm just not that kind of dog. And never will be. Dry land suits me just fine. So you wouldn't find me there right now at her side IN THE WATER, even if she has started crying into the ocean.

I just want to clear that up.)

CHAPTER 62

The next day Danielle and Dr. Johnson, Sam's principal, stand in the school vegetable garden. Dr. Johnson picks ripe tomatoes off the vine while Danielle tries to explain the situation. When she stops speaking he shakes his head.

"I'm not saying it's impossible, Danielle. In fact, I've suspected something … uh … distracting has been going on with your father for a while. It just isn't any of my business as long as it isn't affecting his work."

"But Dr. Johnson -"

"You took quite a chance coming here today, young lady. That kind of trouble could cost a man his

job. Let's pretend this conversation never occurred."
He seems to be dismissing her.

Emboldened, nonetheless, she adds, "You have to
realize that my father's life is more important to us
than his job!"

Johnson bends down to pull some carrots from
the soil in the bed beside the tomato vines.

"Look, Danielle, to be frank, I took a stand when
my music teacher messed around with cocaine. But I
really can't help you here. Your father's functioning.
He's even delivering a winning basketball team."

Danielle turns away but stops and turns back to
face him. "If you think he's so all right, then why
didn't he get the chairmanship?"

Johnson is taken aback but doesn't reply.

Once out of the vegetable garden, Danielle gets
on her skateboard and heads for Nicky's house.

CHAPTER 63

Minnie paces up and down Dr. Prabu's office. He
sits behind his desk, listening to all she has to say,
grinding his teeth. He had been cleaning the snake
tank, and - for the moment - snakes are squirming in
a porcelain bedpan.

*(Ooh, yuck! Grosses me out, those slimy squirmy things! I
never understood the point of a creature with No Hands, No
Legs, No Ears, No Nose, No Eyebrows, No Chin, No Fur, No*

Top, No Bottom. Not even a Tail ... unless you consider the whole thing just a tail with fangs!)

"It sounds too iffy to me," Dr Prabu shakes his head. "If his liver was shot or cirrhotic, that's one thing. If he had peripheral neuritis that's something else."

He unwraps a protein bar and takes a bite, then offers her one.

Minnie shakes her head. "No, thank you, Dr. I've lost my appetite these days."

"If he's nipping a little too much like you say and doing goofball things –"

Seeing that one of the snakes has slithered out of the pan onto the counter, Dr. Prabu stops speaking. He grabs it, puts it back and continues, "- I'd say let him alone. All men go through mid-life crises."

He pins her with both eyes. "Maybe you two could use a little counseling? I could recommend someone."

Minnie gets up to leave, giving Dr. Prabu an imploring look, disappointed that after all that, the only thing he had to offer was a granola bar!

CHAPTER 64

Danielle sits on the brick step leading to Mrs. Harper's back yard. The Doberman is lying beside her, trying to chew on the end of her new skateboard. She knocks him lightly on the snout and he looks up. Her cell phone rings and the dog's ears shoot up. Danielle pulls the phone out of her backpack and answers. It's the volunteer at the dog shelter on the edge of Parkside, calling to tell her that a dog came in the night before that matches the description of Beckett. When can Danielle get there to check it out?

"In twenty minutes," Danielle replies, breathless. "YESSS!!" she yells as she picks up her skateboard, reaching back to pat the disappointed Doberman on the head. "Sorry. But this is more important!"

Once out of the garden she jumps on her skateboard and rides as fast as she can down streets, across town and on to the next town. She's breathing hard when she gets to the shelter that she's checked many times over. She dismounts and races inside.

Juan, the volunteer who has gotten to know her in the past months, is loading sacks of dry cat food onto a shelf.

"Where's Beckett?!" Danielle demands, trying to catch her breath.

"Ah, Danielle. I'll take you. We're all waiting for Godot!"

He smiles at his own wit and leads her into the back where the small kennels are.

At the doorway Danielle pauses. "I'm scared to go, Juan."

"Why?"

"What if it isn't Beckett?"

"Then it isn't Beckett."

"I don't know if I can take the disappointment."

Juan leans against the wall. A chorus of yips and yaps and whines and meows are coming from the rescued animals in back. A large orange cat in a nearby cage reaches a paw out and pats at Juan's shoulder, catching a thread from his shirt in a claw.

Danielle notices and gently unsticks the cat's claw from the fabric.

"Could you look for me? Please Juan?" Danielle pleads.

"Sure. But how would I be positive? It looks just like the posters all over town - a mongrel with lots of terrier and spaniel traits. Cute but a little goofy."

Danielle bites her lip.

"How many ears does it have?"

"Ears? The usual. Two."

"No seriously, go look. If it has two whole ears it's not Beckett. See, Beckett is missing half an ear."

Juan disappears between the kennels. Danielle's hands turn into fists as she listens to the sounds.

Juan calls out, "Two whole ears!" He returns, "Sorry, dude."

She narrows her eyes and turns to go.

"Hey, wait! Why don't you take another one instead? We've got a Shih Tzu and Pekingese and Boxer and even funny little Yorkie, and they all need a good home, ya know."

"I want Beckett back. Period!"

"Don't give up then," Juan pats her shoulder. "Maybe the next one coming in here will be your old pal."

"Yeah. Maybe. But where could she be all this time? Is she even alive? I hate to think …"

(If she only knew! I have now been delegated to an old man dying of heart disease. He is alone with no family. For the moment, I am his family. It's okay, except he has really funny hairy ears like Yoda, as well as medicine-smelling breath.

And they say that we dogs have bad breath!)

CHAPTER 65

Seated on the Hammonds' living room chair, Minnie drinks a cup of tea while Danielle sips a Coke from a straw. Jean reclines on the couch, legs covered with a patchwork comforter. Jeff stands near to the large flat-screen TV.

"Yeah, I've heard of the Pacific Institute," Jeff tells them.

"You have?" Minnie replies with surprise.

"Uh huh. And Alanon, the sister organization to AA, Alcoholics Anonymous," Jeff adds. "I've thought of going but never had the guts."

Jean rolls her eyes toward the ceiling. Irritated, she says, "Don't get on about that, Jeff, you'll drive me to drink."

Jeff ignores her lame joke.

"Why didn't you say something to me before?" Minnie asks.

"I didn't know what to say, I -" Jeff replies.

Jean cuts in, "Oh, Jeffrey, please! Mark my word, Minnie, Sam won't put up with you messing around with his ... his relaxation. I mean, c'mon, I like a few drinks myself. If it came to a choice, booze would win out every time."

Danielle looks pleadingly at Jeff. He walks over and strokes her hair. A ring on his finger gets caught in the long tangles.

"I'll do anything I can to help," he tells her in earnest, untangling his ring. "Count me in."

Jean shakes her finger at Minnie.

"Don't kid yourself, Minnie. Jeff wouldn't really be very happy if I stopped drinking. You see, I'd bore him."

Jean snickers. Jeff shakes his head and squeezes Danielle's shoulder, ignoring his wife's foolishness.

CHAPTER 66

Early evening the following Thursday, Minnie is teaching a tap-dancing class. The students are pre-school age, three and four-year old boys and girls. They require patience. She demonstrates a loud, tricky tap routine since the kids like the sound of the taps on the hard floor. The little ones can't possibly do it but they try anyway, making a comic mess of the dance but plenty of noise.

When the class finishes, Rosa and Minnie help them put on their jackets and wait until each is picked up by a parent or babysitter. After the last has gone, Rosa takes out a red lipstick and brightens her lips. The phone rings. Rose answers, tells Minnie, "It's someone named Rex," and hands her the phone.

"Hi, Minnie," says Rex at the other end of the phone. "I've read the material Danielle gave me."

"And?"

"Enlightening stuff. No, I'm not kidding, I really found it fascinating, in fact. If I can believe it."

"You can believe it."

"It means that I know at least three alcoholics at different stages. That explains a lot of unexplained phenomenon to me, like why my cousin Albert with the highest IQ in the family has been in and out of homeless shelters for years."

"And Sam?"

He sighs. "Sam's different. Perhaps he does have one too many once in a while, but he's the coach. I'd feel like a meddler. He'd never forgive me for …"

"Then you won't get involved?"

"Try to understand where I'm coming from. He's one of my buddies."

Minnie chokes up.

"I'm watching a building burn and everyone's telling me they don't smell smoke," she explains in a trembling voice. "Rex, I'm coming apart over Sam."

"Maybe you should see someone about yourself. Sometimes women's hormones go out of whack -"

She slams down the phone, turns toward the window and presses her forehead against the cool glass.

After a few seconds, she reaches into the desk drawer, takes a cigarette and lights it. Rosa looks at her in shock.

"Minnie, are you out of your mind? I thought you'd finished with that finally!!"

Minnie's shoulders tremble; Rosa gives her a hard hug.

"What shall I do, Rosa? I don't know what to do. The kids are so ... disturbed."

Children begin to arrive for the next class. Minnie wipes her face with a tissue. A teary six-year-old girl taps on her arm.

"I've forgotten my tutu, Mrs. Godot."

Minnie wipes away a tear and forces a smile.

"It's alright, sweetie. You can dance in your jeans today."

CHAPTER 67

(It's been many, many Saturday mornings away from the Godot family and though I enjoy giving kindness and licks to these old people and seeing them smile, it is this time of the week that I truly miss being there at the Godot house.

First, everybody slept a little bit later than usual, and so I got to as well, snuggling with Danielle or Simon, cuddled up under their covers. Ah! Dog bliss!

Second reason is that often Saturday mornings - or sometimes Sundays - meant Bacon-and-Egg Day! Apart from spare rib bones or Minnie's butter cookies, I liked nothing better than

*a scrap of bacon tossed at me from the Godot table. Maybe if
I close my eyes I can imagine I'm there with them ...)*

Simon and Minnie sit at the table while Danielle
stands over the stove wearing a Bart Simpson apron,
frying bacon and scrambling eggs. She's the best
breakfast maker in the family, and always gets a kick
out of being the boss on such occasions, even if she
is not as calm and confident as usual.

Flopsie has her own chair and nibbles a breakfast
of parsley and dill on a small plate while Pickle looks
on hoping he, too, will be given a treat.

*(Now I REALLY wish I were there, too, drooling on the
floor waiting for the extra bits of bacon slipped from behind the
counter when nobody was looking.)*

Simon's stomach produces a loud set of grumbles.
(God, mine, too!)

"It's almost ready, Si," Danielle promises.

Simon taps his toe on the floor.

"Two seconds," Minnie tells him. "She's going as
fast as she can."

"You say two seconds and you mean two minutes,
Mom," Simon grumbles. "Why don't you just say
two minutes?"

"Simon, don't be so *estúpido!*" Danielle snaps while
stirring gooey eggs.

Simon shoots a look at his sister that says, "Cool
it."

"We never have any fun anymore, do we Pickle?"
Danielle mumbles.

The porch door slams shut. Sam's back from his run. He's dressed in running gear, a towel around his neck that is soaked with sweat.

Sam ruffles Simon's hair. He reaches for Danielle's head, but she ducks out from under his hand, intent on her frying pan.

"Yum. That smells good," he comments. "I'd love some eggs. But no bacon, too fatty."

"Fried or scrambled, Dad?"

Sam picks up Flopsie, strokes the silky black fur, and sits down with the rabbit on his lap.

"I don't know, you decide."

Danielle fries two eggs for her father and piles scrambled eggs on the other three plates, adding crispy strips of bacon to these. One by one she brings the plates to the table and places each on a Beckett placemat.

"Why did you fry them, Dani?" Sam asks.

"I thought you didn't care? Dónde estabas, papa?"

"*La playa*. I went to the beach. I got up early and did four miles."

"Aren't you stiff?" Simon wonders in a sarcastic tone of voice.

Sam stretches out his right leg; rubs the knee. "Sure am, but it feels great. No pain, no gain!"

"God, Dad. You say that ALL the time!" Simon moans.

"Well, it's mostly true, son," Sam replies, patting Simon's back.

Danielle deals slices of perfect toast like playing cards to every plate.

Sam pushes his aside. "I've turned over a new leaf, folks. I decided I'm too young to let it all hang out." He pats his belly.

"If my basketball team can make it to the semi-finals, I can shape up. No more burritos. No toast. Plenty of protein and fresh vegetables ONLY." He takes a forkful of egg. "Delicious, you're the best cook. Gracias," he tells Danielle.

To Minnie he announces, "I'm gonna get the drippy faucet fixed. I swear!" and to the whole family he adds, "And ... family ... I'm going on the wagon! That's right, no more drinking. None. Zilch. Nada."

He beams as he says this. Danielle's mouth drops open. Simon shoots a look of shock at his mother. Pickle is waiting for his breakfast treat and ignores the news.

(And me, I am here drooling at the old age home, having to imagine the smell of bacon and buttered toast, and Danielle's excited expression. And I'm not sure I believe Sam. He said he was going to stop before, and always started drinking again.

Translation of a famous saying among us dogs: Never Trust a Master Who Abandons You!)

CHAPTER 68

Simon pedals his bike while ahead of him Danielle skates rapidly across town towards the Pacific

Institute. They're anxious to deliver the good news before it pops like a soap bubble. When they arrive they jump off their assorted wheels and insistently ring the bell.

Harry opens the door and gestures for them to come inside. They see that he's been speaking with a long-haired boy a bit younger than Simon who's got a big black eye and a split lip, so Danielle hesitates before she requests, "Can we speak with you?"

Harry pats the boy's back.

"I'll be right back, Otto."

When they're alone in the hallway with Harry he inquires, "What's up, guys? Is something wrong?"

"It's all off," Danielle bluntly tells him.

"Why?"

"He's gone on the wagon. Our dad! He stopped drinking!"

"So?"

"SO? So how can we do an intervention on someone's who's not drinking?"

"People who don't have a problem don't go on the wagon."

"Well, what should we do?" Simon asks.

"Don't do anything. Let's wait and see. Most alcoholics have periods of control. Let's continue with our preparation for the moment. We can always cancel the intervention if we change our minds."

Danielle nods.

As they're about to shut the door behind them, Harry says, "Danielle?"

"Yes?"

"Um ... do you realize you're wearing a chef's apron? Care to rustle up breakfast for a hungry sober alcoholic counselor?"

Danielle looks down, and sure enough, she's wearing the stupid apron. There are bits of dried egg over Bart Simpson's face. She unties and removes it in a fluster, while Simon and Harry crack up. She knocks Simon on the head and walks ahead, skateboard under her arm.

Simon's hurries to catch up, rubbing his head.

CHAPTER 69

Later that afternoon, Danielle's alone at home. Simon's at Jerry's, and her parents have gone to see a movie. They'd asked her to join them, but Danielle's not into soppy films about falling in love.

She goes into the kitchen and takes an open bottle of wine from the refrigerator, is about to mark the bottle with a black Sharpie, then reconsiders and turns the bottle upside down. She makes a small mark where the line of the liquid falls. Pickle chirps, adding his two cents.

"You don't know it, but you're our family policeman," Danielle says to Pickle.

Pickle stares at her, ruffles up his feathers.

"You need to keep an eye on him. But this is so I can keep track if anybody has drunk any, and they won't know it since who would think of turning the bottle upside down to check the mark?"

She reaches into a cabinet and grabs a string of millet as a treat for Pickle. As soon as she hangs it in the cage Pickle begins crunching millet pellets, discarding the husks out the side of the cage.

Inside the cupboard under the sink are two more bottles of wine, unopened. She shoves them further back, behind a pile of sponges. Along the bottom of the cupboard march a line of black ants. Grabbing a spoon from the drawer, she adds a dollop of honey and holds it under the ants, watching as they walk onto the spoon. When there are about ten ants on the spoon, she places it in Pickle's cage.

"I don't know if you'll like this variety of ant, Pickle. But if you do, here's a snack, and if you don't, perhaps you'll at least have a taste. You know, people eat chocolate-covered ants in some places, like China, I think."

She suddenly remembers that Buddhists don't kill anything, and just when she's about to remove the spoon, the doorbell rings.

It's Mrs. Harper, the nameless Doberman beside her. She's wearing her usual floral bathrobe. Gently held in the jaw of the dog is a bulge of soft black fur, which Danielle quickly recognizes as Flopsie.

"Oh, my God!!"

"Someone must have left the window open," Mrs. Harper tells her. "Peter Rabbit seems to have squeezed out."

Danielle gently pries the dog's mouth open and removes Flopsie. She flicks the dog on the nose, though she feels like doing much more to it!

"Thank you, Mrs. Harper." Remembering her hearing loss, she raises her voice. "And ... ah, it's a she, not a he."

"Sorry, Honey," Mrs. Harper apologizes.

"It's okay. I suppose it only really matters to the rabbit."

"Hmm. Quite right," Mrs. Harper adds as her strong dog yanks at the leash and pulls her back outside.

Danielle closes the front door and puts her head close to Flopsie, her hands cuddling the furry belly. Flopsie's heart is beating wildly.

"Poor thing. It would be like Simon being in the jaws of a dinosaur!"

Feeling something icky, she removes one hand from under Flopsie. It is covered with dog slobber. She wipes the hand on her jeans while carrying Flopsie into the kitchen to rinse her hand at the drippy sink. She takes two small carrots for the rabbit and some grapes for herself from the refrigerator, then goes upstairs to her bedroom where they stretch out on her bed, munching. She's glad to be on her own this afternoon with the rabbit and the calm quiet. More and more she likes to be alone, and worries that maybe she is becoming anti-social.

(Did I hear 'calm'? Did I hear 'quiet'? Not where I am! I gotta sit on some of these old people's laps and listen to CNN

news for hours - Bombs! Hijackings! Serial Killer On The Loose! - or put up with snoring all night until I'm ready to bite off somebody's toe! This is getting serious. If I am not going to be reunited with Danielle and her family, I gotta come up with a Plan B. And soon!)

CHAPTER 70

Sam and Danielle have been playing a video game of football together in the living room all afternoon. It's Sunday, and true to its name, sunlight pours in all the windows as the afternoon lingers. They're having a good time.

"*Más rápido!* Faster, run faster," Danielle half screams, half giggles.

"Darn it. You got me, Dani!"

"Yes!! I'm the champion again! You really suck at this, Dad."

"Yeah, well, we weren't raised on these games like you kids are."

He takes a hand off the gamepad and wiggles his fingers in front of her face. "Our fingers haven't developed the right muscles."

Danielle reaches for Sam's glass, pretends to sip but is really sniffing it.

"Hey! Get your own soda," he snaps.

He pushes the button on his gamepad. Red lights flash on the screen along with blips and bleeps. "Another game?" Sam suggests.

"Sure. You like losing, huh?" Danielle grins.

Simon wanders into the room in his Cub Scout uniform. He eyeballs Sam's glass. "What're you drinking, Dad?"

"Pepsi Light, Si."

Simon looks suspiciously at the glass. "Can I have a taste?"

Sam pushes the glass toward him. "Sure. Have a sip."

Simon takes a sip.

Minnie walks into the room with her knitting basket, and makes herself comfortable on a soft green chair. She watches as Sam and Danielle resume playing and shouting.

"Interception!"

"Pass, don't run. C'mon, c'mon!"

Minnie stares at the glass on the table beside Sam as she removes a big ball of bright purple wool with one quarter of a sweater attached. She reaches her hand down into the basket, but it comes up empty. She searches the basket with both hands, turns it upside down, emptying it out.

She's looks puzzled. "My knitting needles have vanished! They were here just yesterday. That's odd."

Simon shrugs his shoulders and heads for the kitchen.

Sam ignores her. He is concentrating on trying not to get beaten by his eleven-year-old daughter.

Danielle also doesn't answer. She is focused on the screen and the game that she is already winning. Again.

(I just have to make a comment here. I mean, please! It is Sunday, gorgeous out, and they are all inside holding electronic plastic thingys in their hands playing football that is not-really-football. Sometimes you humans act really odd. And, no, it not just because I am jealous that we dogs can't hold game-pads with our paws! Meanwhile on this sunny Sunday, I am outdoors being taken for a walk in the gardens of the Old Age Home by an old lady with blue hair and creaky knees.

The flowers smell lovely, the dog pee on nearby trees even lovelier, and I wonder if I am getting used to my Danielle-less life?)

CHAPTER 71

At the end of the week a light drizzle falls outside the Pacific Institute. Minnie, Danielle, Simon, Jeff and Harry are all milling around inside. After Harry arranges the chairs in a circle, he gestures for everyone to choose a seat. The chair nearest the door is left empty. This is where Sam will sit if and when they do the real intervention.

"What if my dad won't sit down?" Danielle asks Harry.

"Now, what do you think, folks? Is Sam the type that might get up and walk out?"

"I've seen him leave a bridge game in a huff when he's losing," Jeff chuckles.

"And he always makes excuses and gets up when I'm winning at chess," Danielle adds.

Harry laughs. "Perhaps we should seat him furthest from the door. Danielle, would you switch seats, take the seat near the door?"

She does.

"Okay," Harry asks everyone, "Do you all have your lists?"

They each take out a sheet of paper and hold it in their hands. Except Simon.

"No list, Simon?"

Minnie answers for him, "Simon isn't sure that –"

Harry holds up the palm of his hand to stop her. "Let Simon speak for himself."

"I may be mad at him, but I don't want him to be mad at me over this," Simon admits. "I mean … well, he never has hit me or my sister. And he's not drinking now … Maybe he's okay?"

"I understand." Harry tells him, "Just hang in and listen and see how you feel when the time comes. Okay?"

Simon nods.

Harry turns back to the group. "Okay, folks, now, in this pre-intervention role-play, Jeff, why don't you be Sam?"

Jeff moves into Sam's empty chair. He pulls himself up tall, clears his throat and imitates Sam's deep voice.

"Okay, team, seventy-five push-ups, four thousand sit-ups. No pain, no gain."

Danielle snickers.

Minnie clears her throat. "Look, Harry. Simon's right. Sam's been so good lately. I'm having second thoughts, too. It's been peachy since he's been on the wagon - nights with the kids, up early, helping around the house. Also, he's in seventh heaven. You see, his basketball team is going to the finals."

Harry isn't fazed. "No problem. This is just a rehearsal. You can always change your mind."

"Good," Minnie says, relieved.

"And, besides, I don't know if we have enough people with us. It might not be effective with so few. Let's start with you, Danielle. Just read the concerns out loud."

Danielle clears her throat. She brushes her hair out of her eyes, and asks, "Sorry, does anybody have a rubber band?"

Minnie takes one out of her purse and hands it to her. Danielle pulls her hair back into a ponytail and fastens it. Minnie is pleased to see the hair off her face for the first time in a long while.

"Now, then," and Danielle begins reading her list, speaking softly.

"A bit louder, Honey."

She begins again, speaking with a loud voice.

"One: If it hadn't been for you, Beckett would be home with us today. But she disappeared because you were too busy drinking with your Army buddies.

Did she starve? Did a coyote kill her? Two: You inconsiderate jerk, you kept me up many times at night playing your stupid music at full —"

Harry holds up his hand. "Hold on, Danielle. Your list is supposed to present reality to your father that is, one, presented with love and concern, and two, presented with specific data related to his drinking. And three, you tell how you felt at the time, like, 'I felt angry, hurt, ashamed, guilty,' something like that."

"But he DID do those things! I'm not making it up," she protests.

"AND he ruined my Harry Potter card collection," Simon interjects, "spilling his stinky beer all over 'em. And there's some things I'm too embarrassed to tell anyone, yet."

"I'm sure he did everything you say, guys." Harry reassures, "but this is not supposed to be an attack on your father. If you can't eliminate your judgmental attitude, and put your anger aside, none of this will work."

"Judg-men-tal!" Simon says to himself. "What does that mean?"

CHAPTER 72

Danielle stretches across her bed doing homework while Flopsie chews on crumpled-up math notes tossed on the floor. The landline rings. She goes into her parents' room and answers it.

"Hi, who's this?" asks a voice.

"Danielle Godot."

"It's me, Rex Cunningham."

"Oh, hi, Mr. Cunningham."

"I just wanted to tell you that we lost the game."

"Poor Dad. He'll be upset. He was sure he had a winning team."

"Yeah, poor us. Look ..." he takes a breath, "I know your father's been on the wagon."

"Two weeks now. It's great."

"Yeah, well ... uh ... we all felt so grim after the game and ..."

"Yes?"

"We stopped at Mike's Bar, to soothe our wounded spirits."

"Did Dad ...?"

"He had a couple. Now I'm not saying he's a drunk, but ... Listen, please don't tell him I called. I feel like a heel, but would you tell your mother, please."

"If you tell me to I will."

"Good luck, Danielle. I'm sorry," Rex adds, hanging up.

"He's not YOUR your dad coming home to do who-knows-what to who-knows-who!" she says into the phone, knowing there is nobody there to hear her.

Walking back to her room, her breathing becomes a bit spastic. Flopsie looks up, and her nose begins to wriggle faster.

(Animals always know when their people are upset. And me, Beckett, even better and quicker than that dippy rabbit or dorky parakeet. For example, I now know when one of these old people are going to die, and I'll go wander into their room and lie down nearby. It seems to calm them if I'm around, and they die more peacefully.

Okay, Danielle is not going to die, but still, if I were there and had seen her like that, I'd have put my head on her lap and would lie nearby with that sympathy face we dogs specialize in. Or else, I'd run around in circles with an excited look on my face, eyes bulging, tongue hanging out, that means I Wanna Play, just to distract her.)

CHAPTER 73

To try and calm down, Danielle gets into the shower and washes her hair. Wrapping her mother's candy striped bathrobe around herself, she gets out and scrutinizes herself in the mirror. She pulls her mother's large comb through her hair, smoothing out the tangles and makes a ponytail with an elastic band. Locking eyes with herself in the mirror, she scrunches her nose.

"Blah, blah, blah," she mutters, and begins laying sheets of newspaper over the linoleum floor because she's planning to clean out Flopsie's cage. It's humid from all the hot water and the paper sticks.

She leaves to get Flopsie and her cage, then returns. "Calm down. I'm not gonna give you a shower, too."

Sam sticks his nose in the bathroom door. He's morose.

"We lost." He brings his nose to the stop of her wet head. "Hey, glad to see you've finally combed your hair. Ooh, your shampoo smells like bubblegum."

"And you smell too, Dad ... like peppermint."

"No, spearmint, it's a Lifesaver." he tells her, sticking out his tongue to show the half-sucked Lifesaver on it. "Oh, Honey," he moans, "I wanted to win soooooo much! I could taste it."

"Sorry, Dad. Really I am."

Minnie pops in to squirt some cream onto her hands.

"They trounced us, Minnie," he tells her.

Minnie narrows her eyes. "Did you go out with the team to soothe your wounds?"

"Nah. Who felt like company? I came right home. Are we in a rush?"

She, too, smells the mint he's sucking. A look passes between Minnie and Danielle showing they both know he's lying.

"No. We've got plenty of time. Your suit's pressed." She squeezes his hand. "I'm sorry, Sam, sorry about the game."

"Yeah. Me, too. I think I'll lie down for a few minutes."

When she's alone again, Danielle looks up into the mirror and imitates her father's words.

"I came right home. I came RIGHT home, ugh!" she grunts and looks down to Flopsie. "I hate all this lying! How'd you like it if I said 'Oh, Flopsie, dear, I cleaned your cage, I baked you carrot cake, I bought a hundred dollar rabbit shampoo for you' and I hadn't actually done ANY of those things?"

Flopsie's nose just keeps twitching.

CHAPTER 74

Sunset smears peach-pink colors across the sky as they arrive at the theater. Once inside, dressed up in a silky red dress, Minnie bustles around the dressing room helping her young students prepare for their recital. She ties an untied shoe lace, slicks down some stray hair, wipes a tear of stage fright from someone's eyes.

The recital is about to start. Out in the auditorium Sam, Danielle and Simon are combed and neat; they're seated in the front row. The hall is decorated with balloons and red streamers.

The auditorium fills with excited parents, friends, sisters and brothers of the dancers. Finally, the lights dim and the audience settles down. Several coughs and throat-clearing noises pierce the dark. From the side of the stage Minnie peeks nervously out from behind the curtain.

After a moment, the piano can be heard. A bright spotlight hits the stage as the velvety curtain parts to reveal little sugar plum fairy boys, and girls in Heidi dresses.

The audience bursts into applause.

As Danielle watches the performance, she remembers her mother's disappointment that she preferred skating and tree-climbing to taking ballet lessons.

But because the dancing up on stage seems like such fun, Danielle - for the first time in her life - wishes she'd given ballet a try.

CHAPTER 75

After the show, the Godot family piles into the car and drives over to Zorba's. Constantino seats them in their favorite booth.

"Congratulations on the show. I heard it went well!" he compliments Minnie.

"Sorry about the game," he tells Sam. Seeing Sam's hang-dog look at the mention of the game, he puts his arm around Sam's shoulder and suggests, "A drink to start, Coach? It'll cheer you up."

Minnie, Danielle and Simon look at Sam.

"No, thanks."

During the traditional meal of lamb chops and roasted potatoes, Sam hardly speaks. He glances at other tables a lot, noticing how many of them are dotted with glasses of wine or beer.

Simon watches his dad. Minnie does, too. Danielle's silent, just like Sam is. She gathers scraps from the plates and hides them in a paper napkin for Flopsie.

Soon the bouzouki player and singer begin their romantic song on the stage. Sam looks at his watch. The music seems to annoy him. Chewing on juicy lamb chops, all three watch Sam rather than the entertainment. Everyone is edgy.

About ten minutes into the music, Sam raises his hand and calls out.

"Constantino?"

Constantino approaches.

"An ouzo, please." Sam turns defiantly to Minnie. "Want one?"

"Dad!!" exclaims Danielle, "I thought you were on the wagon?"

"I was talking to your mother. Tonight's a special night," he answers.

Danielle feels stung.

He glares at Minnie and repeats the question. "Want one?"

"Okay. One."

Constantino goes to get the drinks. In an instant, Sam is all boyish charm. He turns to Minnie, "Didn't I dress up for the recital?"

He loosens his tie, rolls up his sleeves, turns to his kids. "And aren't I the dad who loves his kids the most in the whole wide world?"

Danielle feebly nods her head. This time it's Simon who is speechless.

The drinks are served.

"Listen, family!" Sam explains gravely, "I can go back on the wagon anytime I feel like it. Honest. And, look, I've already lost a few pounds." He pats his belly. "But, tonight, tonight we deserve to ..." he gestures toward Minnie, "... celebrate how charmingly your mother's little students danced."

He puts one hand on Minnie's shoulder, picks up his glass with the other. He raises it in a salute to Simon, winks at Danielle.

Sam swallows the fiery drink in one gulp and closes his eyes. His face softens as the strong liquid reaches his stomach and the bouzouki music wakes up his senses.

Not bothering to sneak anymore, Danielle grabs chop bones off plates and adds them to her napkin hoard for the Doberman.

(How dare she steal a lamb chop bone for that Doberman when she knows it would have made me dance around in circles!

Instead, for my dinner I got the rejected Velveeta cheese sandwiches from a bingo party. That icky fake-cheese stuff sticks on the roof of my mouth. BLECH!)

CHAPTER 76

Alone on the front sidewalk late on Saturday morning, Danielle cleans her new skateboard. The day before, she and Nicky rode through puddles left by a sudden rainstorm and mud has caked its wheels. She carefully picks the dried mud off with a twig, then flicks off what remains with an old toothbrush. She drips oil onto the axle of each wheel and spins them to spread the oil.

The postman arrives, says "Hi," and gives her a batch of mail. In the pile there's an overstuffed envelope marked EXPRESS MAIL.

Danielle brings the mail into the kitchen, where her mother stands chopping an onion in time to the dripping faucet, tears streaming from her eyes. Liking the onion smell, Pickle is perched on Minnie's head watching every chop-chop, chop-chop.

"Mail!" Danielle says, laying it on the counter. "There's this EXPRESS MAIL letter."

Minnie wipes her hands on a dishtowel and clasps the fat envelope. She rips it open, pulls out airline schedules and assorted travel brochures. Mystified, Minnie examines the tickets and pulls off a white business card attached with a paper clip:

MAX KATZ: SURF TRAVEL.

She glances over at Danielle, who is leaning over the counter, curious and excited.

Minnie picks up her cell phone and dials the number on the card. A lively voice at the other end says, "Surf Travel."

She glances at the business card, "Max Katz, please."

"I'm Max."

"Hi. There's been a mistake. I just received some airline tickets."

"What are the tickets for?"

"They're tickets to Greece. Nice, but we have no plans to go there!"

"Oh. I must have sent them to the wrong address. Sorry, ma'am. They're for customers of mine, planning a once-in-a-lifetime sabbatical trip to Greece - the Godots. If you tell me where and who you are, I'll come by to pick them up."

"Wait, what? The Godots? A sabbatical? Hang on, I'll come over."

"Sure thing, ma'am."

Minnie shakes the chopped onion into a bowl, covers it and places it in the refrigerator. Pickle squawks. She washes her hands, grabs the envelope and her purse and tells Danielle, "I'll be back."

Danielle grabs her red hoodie. "I'm coming with you."

"Danielle."

"Mom!"

"Danielle!"

"MOM!!"

CHAPTER 77

Entering Surf Travel, Danielle stares at pictures on the wall of the Great Wall of China and the Taj Mahal. Minnie hands Max the envelope with the tickets and other materials.

"Sam Godot's a great guy," Max tells them. "He's been planning this trip with me for about two years."

"What does this 'great guy' look like?" Minnie asks.

"Six two, fair haired, well built but gone a little to seed."

He pats his belly and continues, "A little crazy, too. He looks like," he points his finger at Danielle, "you'll look when you're 45."

"Thanks," Danielle mutters.

"How do you mean, 'a little crazy'?" Minnie asks.

"Well, enthusiastic about the trip one day, then I don't hear from him for a while."

"That's rather odd, no?"

"Yeah, and after I don't hear from him, he comes in and begins planning again. Real romantic guy. But then one day I see him on the street and he acts like he doesn't know me!"

He points at Danielle, "You were there. I remember you on a cool skateboard. Remember me?" He opens his shirt a bit and points to his tattoos.

Danielle nods.

Max continues, "Then, not too long after that, he's in here all cut up from a small plane crash, he says … poor guy … again planning away for this trip."

Minnie and Danielle look at each other. Minnie turns back to Max.

"I'm Minnie Godot," she tells him. "Sam is my husband, and he's thirty-eight not forty-five."

"And I'm Danielle. And, yes, he's more than a little crazy. And I'm glad you think my skateboard is cool, but -"

Max puts out his hand, stunned. "Uh … how do you do?"

"Not so well, actually," Danielle replies. She points her finger to one of the posters, says, "See that place?"

Max follows her finger to the Taj Mahal, and nods.

"Wish I was there!"

CHAPTER 78

Hopeless as it seems, Danielle can't stop searching for Beckett. After school she and Nicky skate to an animal shelter two towns away. The employees there know her, and lead them down the corridor. She and Nicky examine all the newest arrivals. Several are in sorry states from battering or starvation or being lost over long periods of time. As always, her spirit sinks when she doesn't see Beckett's face and half-ear among the new faces.

(I want to bark loudly, but I know she'll never hear me. So every day now I close my eyes and send her messages with my mind - "I'M ACROSS TOWN AT AN OLD AGE HOME. COME FOR ME" - but she doesn't hear me. Or she's not really listening inside. Or psychic telepathy is hogwash.)

Danielle's notices a pathetic brown and white Beagle most of whose fur has fallen out due to ring worm. Feeling sorry for it, she reaches down to give it a little head rub. As she does, a scruffy gray Bulldog snarls and leaps at her. The dog frightens her, frightens the Beagle, frightens Nicky, too.

Danielle pulls back. "Hey, HELP! There's a crazy dog attacking us!!"

She and Nicky back away slowly, holding their skateboards up like shields. While a worker calms the Bulldog, they reach the doorway.

Back on the street Nicky shakes his head. "God, what a maniac that one was!" he says. "He almost bit you. And ... Ew! You're pretty stinky from petting those dirty dogs."

She smells her hands. "Gross!"

She has second thoughts about the hostile dog.

"I'm sorry for that poor dog, though. I bet it was beaten or starved or something. Otherwise, why would he have snarled at us like that? Dogs aren't born mean, after all."

"I guess. Hey, sorry about not finding Beckett in there," Nicky says.

"Yeah, this has gotten really grave. And demands some new strategy." She pulls a Sharpie out of her backpack.

"Whatcha gonna do?"

"How much money do you have on you, Nicky?"

He puts his hands in both pockets.

"Four dollars and twenty-eight cents," Nicky answers. "Why?"

"I've got seven forty-one, two, three ... that makes ... um, eleven dollars and seventy-one cents. Let's make it even – eleven seventy. We're gonna offer a reward for anybody who finds Beckett. Let's go add it to all the posters."

(Eleven seventy! Did I hear her correctly? Is that all she can come up with for a reward? For MOI? She spends more than that on a new skateboard wheel, and Nicky buys DVDs for twice that! I mean, really! I'm not as important as "Ironman 3" in Blu-ray??)

CHAPTER 79

A week passes. At the beginning of the following one, after school, after Nicky has demonstrated how much cleaner ollies and nollies look on his new skateboard and they've gone their separate ways, Danielle almost doesn't hear her cell phone ringing. Finally she does and pulls it out of her backpack just in time. She hopes it's not a call about her father. There's a strange old man's voice at the other end.

"Are you the owner of a small dog with only half an ear, the one on those 'Missing' signs?" the voice asks.

Her heart stops. Can it be true? "Yes. Yes! I am. Why? Have you found her?"

"Found her! She's been lying on my bed and watching CNN with me for the past two weeks. I'm a resident at the Sunrise View Senior Home and your dog has been here for a couple months now. I recognized her face on one of your posters yesterday when I was being taken out in my wheelchair. There's something about a reward on the poster?"

"Oh, my God! BECKETT!"

"The name's Vince Tucker, not Beckett."

"No, sorry, Beckett is the name of my dog."

"Well, it's not anymore. Folks around here been calling her Jasmine."

"I don't care what her name is, I'm coming over, right NOW! Where are you, please?"

Danielle memorizes the street address, and without even calling home, races toward the Sunrise View Senior Home on Bismark Street on the far edge of town.

When she finds it she leaps off her skateboard and runs in, sweaty and breathless. Inside at a reception desk she asks for Mr. Tucker. Given his room number, she dashes down the carpeted corridor, past room after room of old people in beds, on walkers or sitting in wheelchairs, until she finds the right number. At the open door she sees a frail old man folded up under sheets and blankets, his mouth quivering open and closed, his pale grey eyes staring at a TV in a cabinet. The TV is off.

"Mr. Tucker?" she asks moving closer. "I'm the owner of the dog, of, um, Jasmine. You called me."

"Oh, yes. Jasmine. Cutest little whippersnapper. Used to lick the soup off my face when I was done eating."

"Yes, well, where is she? I mean, right now?"

"Can't say. Don't know. Haven't seen her in … Shucks, I miss my little Jasmine."

"But you said she was on your bed every day. Watching CNN with you, remember?"

"Yes. So she was. Everyday … Did I tell you she used to lick the soup off my face?"

"Mr. Tucker, please. Was she … Jasmine, was she brown and white, short little tail, the left ear half gone?"

"That's her. You forgot to mention her tongue. Why, she used to lick −"

"Where did you last see her, Mr. Tucker? Please!" Danielle cuts in.

"Last saw her … last saw her … well, right HERE on my bed."

"And when was that?"

"What's today?"

"Today is Tuesday," Danielle replies, beginning to get frustrated.

"No, I mean is it turkey with giblets for lunch or beef stew?"

"That I don't know. But -"

"What about that reward? Eleven seventy, wasn't it?"

"When she's in my arms you'll get your reward, I promise," she tells him and impatiently hurries back to the reception desk.

The young woman dressed in white with a badge that says, "HELLO my name is Cynthia" looks up.

"Did you find Mr. Tucker's room okay?"

"Yes, but now I'm looking for a scruffy dog, half an ear missing. I was told she was here."

"Oh, you must mean Jasmine. Great little dog. So cuddly and cute. And she gave so much joy to all the people here. Tragedy that she ran off like she did."

"Ran off! Where? When?"

"Yesterday. Our janitor left the back door open and when Jasmine was on her free time between patients she must have got out. We haven't seen her since. Terrible loss. The folks miss her so much. Why were you asking about her, Honey?"

"Because she was MY dog before she was your dog. And her name is Beckett, not Jasmine! She probably ran off to look for me."

"No need to shout at me!"

Danielle hasn't heard her, and walks slowly away. When she's outside again she slams her skateboard down on the pavement.

"BECKETT JASMINE BOBOLINA, WHERE ARE YOU????" she yells up into the sky.

CHAPTER 80

Minnie pulls her car over to the side of the road and gets out. She's beside a wetland from which sea birds noisily rise up and land. With a shaky hand, she punches a number into her cell phone.

"Harry, it's Minnie. Listen, I … What if we're making a mistake here? Maybe Sam and I just need to use those tickets and go to a Greek island alone and…"

Harry's reply seems to go on forever. Pelicans fly over the sea near the shoreline. As she listens, the birds disappear.

"I understand, yes. But … Listen, I'm on the road, on the way to pick up the kids. Then we're going to … tell him. Harry, my heart is thumping like mad. What if he leaves us?"

She listens, but interrupts. "-Let him drink us all into the ground, at least we'll still have each other!"

Again she is silent for a long while. When she speaks, her voice is childish. "I know it's my decision. Why do I have to make all the decisions? I'm not strong."

She holds up her hand and looks at her gold wedding band glinting in the sunlight. "Sam's supposed to be the strong one. My … my stomach is in knots …"

She presses the ring to her lips. "I mean, what happened to 'For better or for worse' in our wedding vows?"

CHAPTER 81

Inside the gym, Sam watches his basketball players make bank shots. He paces up and down at the edge of the court, occasionally blowing his whistle, calling out to a player.

"If you don't hustle, you don't start," he shouts, blowing the whistle louder, finally getting the players' attention.

"This is team basketball, not hog city! Let's see some blocking, not just layups."

Outside, Minnie's car pulls into the school parking lot. In it are Minnie, Simon and Danielle.

"I wish you could do it, Danielle."

"Mom, I'm the kid."

"Simon?"

"I'm the other kid!" he says from the back seat.

Minnie takes a compact out of her bag, dabs at her make-up. She looks at Danielle imploringly. Danielle shakes her head.

"Mom, I can't!"

"Well, I'm a kid here, too, when it comes to this!" she says, then takes a deep breath and gets out of the car.

She crosses the parking lot, walks through several corridors to the gym and stands at the edge of the basketball court watching Sam with the players. After a long look she moistens her lips.

"Sam!"

He sees her, smiles, and blows his whistle. "Okay, guys, how about some jump shots. I'll be right back."

He strides over to where she's standing. He's grinning. "What're you doing here, what a nice surprise."

"Are you free after practice today?" she asks stiffly.

"Sure."

What she says sounds rehearsed, which it is. "I've made an appointment for us today at a 'family institute' at five when you finish practice. It's regarding some problems -"

His eyes widen. "You've what?"

"- problems regarding our family. I expect you to show up. Here's the address." She hands him a folded sheet of paper.

"You're not serious?"

"I am. Very."

His eyes narrow. "We keep our problems to ourselves in our family."

"Just be there, Sam. We'll be waiting."

"WE? You've involved the kids in this?"

"The kids ARE involved, Sam." She turns and hurries away.

"Minnie," he calls after her, "This isn't right, it's … Minnie!"

She ignores him and keeps on walking. He looks at the sheet of paper. Reading out loud he says, "Pacific Institute."

He lowers himself onto a bench beside the basketball court, digging his shoe into the wood floor, not paying any attention to the action on the court.

When practice finishes, Sam drives along the Coast Road. Faster traffic passes him, leaving his old Saab behind. The sea is calm, mirroring perfectly the blue sky with a few smudges of cloud.

Sam's mind, though, is not calm. Waves of anxiety rise and crash. He is not sure where he is driving to and where he will end up, or if he should stop and have a drink or two or three to fortify himself.

After all, he recalls, there's the nicest little bar just up the road.

CHAPTER 82

Gathered in the conference room at the Pacific Institute are Minnie, Danielle, Simon and Jeff. All except Jeff look gloomy. The door to Harry's private office is open and the sound of Harry speaking on the phone can be heard.

"I know what your mother wants, Otto, and what he wants. But what do YOU want?"

Danielle wonders what other drama may be going on in another family.

Max Katz appears at the door, and Minnie rises to greet him. She introduces him to Jeff and Simon. Danielle is again mesmerized by Max's many tattoos - the jet plane on his forearm, the train circling his neck, the motorcycle on his wrist - and for a brief moment forgets why they are there.

Harry enters the room and looks around. He's wearing a tie and jacket. He taps on the light switch.

"Let me turn some light on the subject," he quips.

No one laughs.

He strolls over to Danielle who's already seated. "You okay, Kid?" he asks her.

She's sunk down in the chair. "Yeah, thanks," she says, half-truthful, half-lying.

The others sit down. Harry consults his watch.

"It's five on the dot, folks."

"I wonder if he'll show up," Danielle says.

Minnie chews her lower lip. Simon is rigid with expectation.

"Have you explained our method to Max?" Harry asks Minnie.

Max nods, "Yes. I just hope I can help."

Danielle is drawing a circle with her foot on the rug. Her shoe drags deeper and deeper along into the pile. She looks over at Simon and notices that his eyes are huge. Turning, Danielle sees her father looming large at the door. Her eyes widen, too.

"Dad!"

His face is as hard as a fist. With a scathing tone of voice he glares at Minnie. "I've obeyed your summons, Madam. Now, tell me what this is all about so we can quickly return to the privacy of our home."

Sam takes in the assembled group. "Jeff!"

Seeing Max he asks, "Who are you?"

Danielle looks beseechingly at Harry. Harry goes over to Sam, puts out his hand.

"I'm Harry Harding. I'm a counselor here at the Pacific Institute."

Sam ignores the hand held out to him.

"They're here out of concern for YOU, Sam."

Sam doesn't react and Harry continues: "If you'll come in, we -"

Sam cuts him off. "This is crazy. My life is nobody's business."

Harry speaks calmly. "All we ask, Sam, is that you sit down and listen to what each person has come here to say to you."

"Say? Say to ME?" Sam replies angrily. "I have a few things to say to them, the rats." He glares at Minnie who flinches.

Harry indicates the empty chair. "We ask you to listen to each person here, one by one. You can have your say afterwards. Is that agreeable?"

"Do I have a choice?"

"You always have a choice, Sam," Harry replies.

There is a heavy pause; the air is thick with anticipation. Finally Sam walks forward and fills the empty seat. Danielle stops holding her breath.

CHAPTER 83

"Seems like a conspiracy," Sam glares at Harry and the circle of faces. "And how dare you mix my kids up in this!"

The tension in the room crackles. Hearing her father speak so harshly, Danielle winces.

(If only I were sitting at her feet to lick her hand. Well, cowering at her feet since it seems like Sam's about to blow!)

"We'll start with Jeff."

Everyone turns towards Jeff, who confidently unfolds his list, then puts on reading glasses.

"Within the past year on the following dates, Sam, you drank five or more drinks in my presence. May 4th and 19th, June 3rd, July 4th, September 9th..."

"So precise. What, no August dates?" Sam quips.

"We were away in August," Jeff replies.

He continues, "September 18th, October 15th, December 9th. On September 18th, after approximately three Bloody Marys you stumbled against the barbecue and burnt your wrist. On October 15th, after approximately five Bloody Marys you walked into my patio door, shattering the glass. Amazingly you escaped with only minor cuts. You might have been blinded or slit your major arteries! This occasion frightened me greatly. As a friend who cares, and as a doctor, I ask you to seek help."

Jeff folds up the paper. Sam looks down at the tip of his shoes for a moment, and then at Jeff, his face a mask. Harry nods at Max.

"Hey, wait a sec. I've never seen that tattooed joker before in my life," Sam says.

"You sure have and I can prove it," Max answers. "Sam, you're a great guy and whether or not you remember me, we've shared an … uh … acquaintance."

"We've what?"

"Drinking can cause blackouts," Harry interjects. "Blackouts are periods of amnesia when a person functions but doesn't remember anything."

"We figured out that sometimes after drinking you would visit Max at the travel agency while you were in a blackout," Minnie explains.

Sam remains bewildered. "Blackouts?"

Max continues: "For two years you and I have worked on sabbatical travels for you and your family, something you wanted to surprise them with. We've agonized over the itinerary; taken great care with boats and house rentals. A few weeks ago you phoned and told me that you were ready to go, that I should finalize the arrangements for a trip. So I have."

Max removes the envelope from his jacket pocket. He fans out the tickets, schedules and other papers. "Have a look for yourself," he continues. "We put together a fabulous Greek island trip."

Max hands Sam the tickets. Incredulous, Sam examines them.

"Get help, Sam!" Max begs.

Harry turns to Minnie. "Minnie, your turn."

There's sadness in Minnie's voice as she begins to speak. "Sam, whatever you think, I love you. That's been one of the problems with all this. Everyone loves you!"

She fights back tears as she unfolds her list.

"You had eleven absences from work last year, four on Mondays after drinking all weekend. I'm ashamed of the way I phoned your school and lied for you. Your late night music marathons disturb and upset me and the kids. Often I've felt lonely and hurt, going to bed alone while you continue to drink. Drinking can explain many of your recent medical symptoms - high blood pressure, poor concentration, poor memory. I'm fearful and frustrated by the toll it's taking on your health and I'm also sure that if something weren't sapping your spirits you'd have more ambition at work and would have gotten the chairmanship."

Minnie's voice grows stronger.

"You seem to be spending more of your free time drinking - on weekends, even school nights. You gave wine to the kids at Zorba's. That upset me. Then you were loud and obnoxious, and when you got on the stage and danced, I felt utterly embarrassed by you. Not because you danced, but because you could hardly stand up. Recently, when you asked Danielle to put the stopper in the tub for you, I realized you were experiencing free-floating fear, which we learned is another symptom of drinking. I felt hopeless and helpless about what drinking was doing to our whole family and guilty about losing you to it."

She looks tenderly at Sam.

"There. It's been said. The secret's out. Drinking is diminishing you, Sam. I can't silently stand by any longer. I would like you to get help."

"And there it is - PLOP! - as big as the room, as big as an elephant!" Danielle mutters to herself.

"What elephant?" Simon leans in and asks, having heard her muttering.

CHAPTER 84

"Simon," Harry calls out.

Simon begins to tremble. His face turns red and tears are welling up in his eyes.

Harry reaches over and squeezes his shoulder. "It's okay, Simon," Harry says. "You don't have to speak if you don't want to. We can come back to you later, if you wish."

Simon meekly nods.

"Okay, then. Danielle?"

Danielle chews on her lip. She takes a deep, long breath and looks directly at her father. Images of Beckett are racing in and out of her mind. She tries to push them away to focus on WHY Beckett was lost, not that she was.

"Dad, I ... there are so many things to say. I've been upset by the very loud music late at night. It would wake me and scare me."

Her voice is measured.

"You've broken so many promises, Dad - promising to help with my homework, work on my skateboard with me, take us to the pier, then changing your mind to drink instead. You put me down in front of Nicky. I was embarrassed when you were wandering around the house in your I-Love-Greece boxer shorts while he was visiting. When you were drinking that night on the pier you broke a promise to get us home by eight. I felt angry and disappointed, like I couldn't trust you."

Sam's knees are trembling.

"Later, when you were driving and put my hands on the wheel, I was so scared, I thought we were all going to die. But the biggest thing of all was when you forgot Beckett in the dog park. When you lost her I wanted to run away from home. I felt so terrible … and … I hated you. I didn't want to be close to you, anymore. When I notice how bad you felt, how you'd still buy dog food, I felt sick at the same time."

Tears slide down her cheeks.

(If I were there, I'd be applauding! That is, if dog paws could clap. Go, Danielle, go!)

"Dad, you … you were always my hero … really … but now, I don't want to be like you, although sometimes I'm afraid I WILL be like you."

Sam's cheeks redden.

"I love you, Dad. But when you drink I don't want to be your daughter. Dad, please get help!"

His face still flushed, Sam is visibly deflated. He stares at Danielle, his first-born child, and his eyes moisten, too.

A slide show of memories scrolls across his mind: of the day Danielle was born and it seemed like his heart would explode with the wonder of it all; of the gleam in her eyes when she first said "Daddy" at age one; of her first lopsided walk across the living room floor; of her first day at school wearing a pale yellow dress that she had chosen herself; of her little hand at age five pointing at a skateboard in a shop window; of how she'd cuddle up to him when he read her stories in bed at night; how, since she was very little, she'd feed squirrels and wild kittens on the side of the road and care for any and all dogs; of her joy to be up in the tree-house he built when she was seven; of the many times they'd lie on their backs out on the lawn at night looking up at the millions of twinkling stars, she telling him the names of the constellations and galaxies she'd learned from a book; and of how protective he felt, carrying her sleeping body up the stairway to bed, so trustingly she clung to him.

Sam continues staring at Danielle, realizing that soon she'll be a teenager, and before much longer, a woman, and his little girl will no longer exist. There's a big lump in his throat.

He and Danielle stare across the room at each other, eyes penetrating into eyes, both teary.

Harry gestures to Simon. "Okay, Simon, how about you, now?"

Simon's chin is pulled downward, he bravely mutters.

"I agree with everyone. Dad, you sometimes act like someone else and it scares me. It really made me mad when you spilled beer on my cards. And, worst of all, you forgot to send the money for our Scouts outing!"

He glares at Sam, then melts. "Dad, I wish you were like before. Our family was really good then."

"Thanks, Simon," Harry says, turning his focus onto Sam.

"Sam, you've heard what each of them has to say. Remember, these are people who love you. They're concerned."

("Wait! Wait!" I want to say. "What about me? What about the dog? Don't I get to say something here? Like, gosh golly, Mr. Godot, you're a really cool guy most of the time, but when you drink that stinky stuff you start doing dumb things, like forgetting to feed me, like stumbling across the living room floor which, HELLO! I AM SLEEPING ON, and tripping over me or stepping on my tail or kicking my stomach, or taking me out for a walk and not even noticing when my leash gets tangled up with a tree trunk until I gag, and worst of all - need it be repeated? - when you forgot about me at the park that Most Terrible of Days. I thought you guys loved me. You broke my heart. You broke Danielle's heart.")

Sam looks at Danielle, then Simon. They're both trying to seem strong, and it pains him. Here are his kids who had the guts to come here today and try to rescue him. "So who is the parent and who is the kid now?" he wonders.

He looks over at Minnie, his beloved wife for fourteen years. "What do you want me to do?" he asks her.

She answers, "Sam, if you agree that drinking is causing you problems, there's a treatment center in Darrow Beach with a good record of recovery. Then there's AA afterwards, Alanon for us. Harry recommends that you go immediately. In fact, we have a reservation for you this evening. I've even packed a bag for you."

For the first time Sam notices his green wheeled suitcase standing in a corner of the room.

Danielle crumbles up the paper she had written her list on and drops it into the wastepaper basket. Simon notices, stands up, and does the same with his list. All the while, Sam watches his kids and his eyes follow the upsetting lists as they become trash in a basket.

CHAPTER 85

Before he softens any further, Sam begins to have second thoughts. He tries to imagine sitting on his porch without a cool, refreshing beer after work and can't. He implores his daughter, "Dani, honey, you know I can take it or leave it alone."

Danielle sternly shakes her head. "No, Dad," she mutters.

Sam turns to Minnie. "I don't beat the kids or you. I've never had an accident or a fight. I've never lost a job or a friend."

"Those are the 'yets'," she tells him. "Drinking is progressive."

Sam winces.

"If you continue to drink," Harry interjects, "I guarantee you'll do all the things you mentioned. It will take everything you love from you."

"But … this just isn't the right time," Sam blurts out. "Basketball season's finishing up. Soon there'll be baseball … There's just no way."

"Sam, please," Jeff interjects. "There will NEVER be a right time."

Harry nods. "Take it from me."

Sam stubbornly shakes his head. "I'm sorry, watching a game on TV without a beer? No Bloody Marys on a Sunday? Heck. I'm just too young to be an alcoholic. Don't you see?" he implores Minnie.

She shakes her head.

He looks at Simon. "Can't you see my side?"

Simon looks away.

Sam begs Danielle. "Danielle, honey, stick up for me. You know me better than anyone."

Danielle pins him with her eyes. "Papa, por favor. Can we go outside and talk alone?"

Sam looks at Harry.

Harry nods. "Why don't you and Danielle step into the garden out back for a few minutes?"

Danielle leads Sam out of the conference room.

As soon as they're out of earshot, Jeff loosens his tie, sighs despondently.

"Jeez, that was tough," Minnie sighs.

"Jean said this would happen," Jeff blurts out.

Max looks at his watch and gets up. "Forgive me, but I've got to run."

He looks sadly at Simon. "I'm sorry I wasn't more help," then he squeezes Minnie's shoulder, "Good luck, folks."

He leaves.

"At least we presented a united front," Minnie comments to Harry.

"You were courageous, Minnie," Jeff tells her, trying to buck her up.

Minnie turns to Harry, asks, "Was it like this for you?"

"Me? Nine years ago I was drinking a gallon of rotgut wine a day. I lived in a seedy hotel on skid row."

Harry on skid row? Everyone's surprised.

"I was thirty-eight years old but in my mind I was still sixteen, thumping a basketball up and down the courts. I was still a high school kid, a basketball star, who just needed the right break to get into pro ball. I'd lie in my room, sucking on my jug and dreaming of the Lakers. Sure, I'd been married and had kids. I'd been an x-ray technician but when it all got too much for me, I walked out and my wife took the kids back home to New Hampshire. If I could come back from skid row, anyone can. Don't lose hope. But it's got to come from him."

The small group is sad but determined while they wait for Danielle and Sam to return.

("Wait, wait, let 'em wait!" I've been waiting nearly six months for Danielle and Sam! I've gone from being called Bob-olina to Beckett to Jasmine, and now I'm back to being just plain old "dog", as in "Get away from here, dog!" or "Hey, dog, don't you have a home?"

"No, I Do Not!" I want to tell them. "Take me! Take me!" You think they listen? You think they care? I'm hanging out on some beach, scrounging for scraps after all the day-trippers have left, and though sand makes a soft mattress, those pesky sand-fleas are bothering me something fierce.

And I am starting to accept that I will NOT be going back to the Godots'. And NOT be Danielle's best friend ever again. But I am hopeful. There are lots of good people out there, and one day one of them - or maybe five! - will take pity on me and take me home.

It WILL happen! I know it!

Plus, I don't really even care what name they call me as long as there are cuddles. Oh, and food!)

CHAPTER 86

Sam and Danielle silently walk through the garden attached to the Pacific Institute. There's a tree filled with ripe yellow lemons, also there are red geraniums, crimson bougainvillea, and a bench painted grey near a tree filled with ripe yellow lemons. Several rotting lemons lie on the ground at the base of the tree. Fluttering above these rotting fruits, a cloud of tiny purple butterflies. In unison, Sam and Danielle notice the swarm and mutter, "Wow."

Danielle sinks down onto the bench and Sam bends to sit beside her, almost crushing a spotted pink and brown lizard neither has seen that's sunning itself. The lizard dashes away.

Sam stretches out his long legs. He pulls a tin of mints from his pocket. He takes one for himself and then offers her one.

She takes it. "Gracias, Papa."

For a few seconds they suck on their mints and say nothing.

Finally, Sam leans toward his daughter. "Honey, I'm so sorry you had to go through this."

The knot in her stomach is still there because she has more to say.

"Dad, there's something I need to tell you. A secret."

"I'm listening."

She chews on her lip. "You'll hate me, like I hated you when you forgot Beckett."

"Do you still hate me?" he asks putting an arm over her shoulder.

"No. I tried to. But I guess I care for you more than I hated you and the caring seems to have burned away the hate, somehow."

"So try me with your secret."

She speaks with a small voice. "Dad, I'm the one that's taping up the knives and scissors. I'm the one who is hiding the sharp knitting needles."

He raises an eyebrow. "But why?"

"I don't know, Dad. I just felt like something bad was going to happen in our house. Like something was coming to hurt us."

He's speechless.

"There's more."

"Tell me."

"I stole an onion from the market for Flopsie. And … here's the worst … I gave two of Mrs. Harper's Doberman dogs away to Nicky to keep. He really wanted dogs and Mrs. Harper is so forgetful, she didn't even notice when I took three for a walk and only came back with one."

"Did you really?" he asks, unable to resist smiling.

"Yeah, I did. And she hasn't even noticed. She just washed up the extra bowls and erased their existence."

Seeing his smile she smiles too.

"I guess we can call that real forgetfulness," Danielle adds. "I mean, imagine - your own dogs!"

The smile fades from Sam's face. "I … it's not much different than what happened with me and Beckett."

Tears fill Danielle's eyes.

"Oh, Sweetie, I wish there were some way I could make it up to you. I really do miss her."

"Me, too, and I always will."

He hands her his handkerchief and she blows her nose.

"I've got to admit, I'm beginning to think she might be gone for good," Danielle confesses. She blows her nose again, pulls at her unruly hair, "And it's time for a haircut."

Sam nods and leans down and plants a kiss on top of her head.

"Daddy?"

"What?"

"I think you should go to this place. Really."

A pained look crosses his face. "Really?"

Danielle climbs up onto the bench and picks a ripe lemon from a branch. She holds it out toward her father.

"Really, Dad. I think you should 'Give The Lemon Aid' just like you once explained to me. Before…"

She points down at the rotting lemons on the ground that are gooey, brown and decomposing.

Her eyes meet his. "*Por favor*. Please, Dad, do it for Beckett."

Blinking his eyes, Sam notices the crisp blue sky, the vast open space above him with limitless possibilities.

Danielle does, too.

Sam turns to Danielle, reaches out, and takes the ripe, bright yellow lemon that's being offered to him.

THE END

BECKETT'S EPILOGUE

That's the story. That's what happened.

I wish I could tell you that there was a happy Hollywood ending, where we were reunited and ran in slow motion through a barley field at sunset into each other's arms. Didn't happen. But that's okay, now. Things worked out in unexpected ways.

Big Sam DID go to rehab, DID stop drinking, DID go to AA and change his life. Once he stopped drinking, the free-floating fear that permeated the family slowly dissipated, that anxious feeling of impending doom that rattled even the passive Buddhist parakeet, Pickle, went away. The family DID go to Greece for the great adventure, but not for another year.

Oh, and Sam did finally fix the drippy faucet. But, silly as it sounds, the day after he did, the kitchen light began to flicker and now Minnie's waiting for someone to get around to fixing that or will do it herself.

It took a while for Danielle to feel really good about things again, but by the next year she and Nicky had competed for and won spots in a Skateboarding Championship that took place over a weekend in another state. Sam drove them there and they camped overnight and Sam taught them how to fish. Neither of them won, but they had a lot of fun, and learned some new stunts from expert skateboarders. Oh, and Danielle asked for and got a surfboard for her twelfth birthday and joined the other surfers riding the waves. Nicky did, too.

And what about me, Beckett, the lost dog, you ask? Long story. But I'll give you the short version.

You see, after I ran away from the Senior Home, and ended up on the beach, I began hanging around a gas station on the

Coast Road. *The funky couple that owns it began feeding me, and pretty soon, they fell in love with me and me with them. I became Número Uno at the gas station.*

They even fed me organic gourmet kibble from Whole Foods. Not knowing my name is Beckett, they began calling me (don't laugh), Cuddles. It took a little while, but slowly I've come to fit the name or the name has come to fit me - anything but Bobolina!

Of course, I'll never forget the Godot kids - Danielle and Simon - and the fun we had that sometimes included a black rabbit who never stopped pooping and a stuffy, depressive parakeet.

In fact, every once in a while, I even see one or all of the Godots drive by on the Coast Road. Last week I saw that they had a new dog with them, a mangy looking, caramel-spotted Dachshund drooling out of the window. (Yuck. Stupid Dachshunds!)

It hurt a little to know I'd been replaced but I was glad the family has survived Sam's problem intact, after those who love him had the courage to corner him and make him face up to what he was doing. I admire them for that.

I hope Sam stays well and, though I hate to admit it, I hope he never forgets that drooling Dachshund in a dog park.

AUTHOR'S NOTE

Dear Reader,

The subject of this book is one close to my heart. I even had a best friend named Nicky with whom I had many great sleepovers. A few years ago we met again and rekindled our friendship. The only difference now is that he likes me to call him Nick, not Nicky. Although the characters in this story are fictional, the devilish main character -alcoholism - is quite real. You see, in many ways it's my own story because - a confession, please keep it to yourself like Beckett's first name, Bobolina - although I have been sober for quite a long time, I am an alcoholic, like Sam.

Once an alcoholic, always an alcoholic. There are wet ones and dry ones. I'm a dry one. I haven't had a drink in a long time and take advantage of a well-known support group to keep me that way because, if I took even one drink, I'd quickly revert to my old ways. If I drank again I would probably be crumbled on the bathroom floor puking and not sitting in a room looking out at the sea, telling you this story.

Alison Leslie Gold

CO-AUTHOR'S NOTE

Alison and I have known each other for a long time — we met on a small Greek island seventeen years ago when she asked me to whitewash her house (sort of like painting walls with milk, except it doesn't get sour and stinky), and slowly discovered that we have a lot in common: we both like traveling and silly movies and dark chocolate and English teatime at four pm and going for walks and believing in human (and animal!) rights and that all girls and boys should try to be who they really are and not what their society or other people expect them to be.

We also like to write about what's important to us, and we both have had our lives touched by alcoholism.

Mine was regarding my father, who would sometimes come home with a weird, droopy look on his face from drinking too much. Luckily, like Danielle's father, he never really got aggressive or violent, but it did cause disruptions in the family and confusion for us kids. Also luckily, my father decided to stop drinking when I was ten years old and has been sober ever since.

So when Alison sent me an unfinished story she had been working on about a family slowly coming to terms with an alcoholic father and asked if I'd help write it, I accepted at once and was grateful, and thought that perhaps I could add some insight into how it feels to be a kid (like Danielle and Simon) with an alcoholic parent ... and about living with pets, because we always had dogs and cats and rabbits around when I grew up.

And we assigned each an astrological sign and a religion.

And, yes, we had names for their poo.

Darin Elliott

RESOURCE LIST

National Council on Alcoholism - informational resource in the U.S. or its equivalent in other parts of the world

Alcoholics Anonymous - a support group where all who might have a problem with alcohol are welcome, found almost everywhere in the world in any phone book or online

Alanon - for teens and friends of alcoholics

Alateen - for teen children and friends of alcoholics

Reputable intervention facilities - contact the National Council on Alcoholism or your guidance counselor or social worker or another expert on alcoholism for a referral.

**GET HELP IF SOMEONE YOU CARE ABOUT IS HAVING TROUBLE WITH ALCOHOL OR DRUGS!!!
IT'S NOT AFFECTING JUST THEM, IT'S AFFECTING YOU, TOO!!!**

ACKNOWLEDGEMENTS:

Alex Calothis and Oneiro Press, U.K., with appreciation.

Hanaan Rosenthal and TMI Publishing, USA with gratitude.

Helle Valborg Goldman, editor, proofreader whose heart is always in the right place.

Gail Vanderhoof, proofreader with a pure heart.

Jean-Noel Lavesvre, artist, illustrator of cover, whose heart runneth over.

Thor and Talia Gold, for help along the way, who is all heart.

Siena Barr, for thoughtful young reader's feedback.

Frank Sabatté and St. Mary's on the Lake, for hospitality and silence on Lake George.

Danielle Durkin, always true blue and bright sage.

My life-long friend Nick and his partner Jerry, for unconditional friendship.

Rick Hernandez, who did for me what Harry did for the Godot family.

Penelope, Sergio, Peaches, Sammy on 23rd Street, all great dogs.

RIP dear Sammy from LA - Thor and Talia will never forget you.

RIP dear Sammy (another dog, and a Special Blend) AKA Samuel Jakob Moses, Jewish & a Libra - the co-author and his brother and two sisters grew up with him, and he was THE best dog ever.

ABOUT THE AUTHORS

Alison Leslie Gold's nonfiction writing on the Holocaust and World War II has received special recognition. Her works include *Memories of Anne Frank: Reflections of a Childhood Friend*, written for young people about Hannah "Lies" (pronounced "lease") Goslar, Anne Frank's best friend, and *Anne Frank Remembered, The Story of the Woman Who Helped to Hide Anne Frank*, written with and about Miep Gies, who hid Anne Frank and rescued Anne's diary. Both of these books have been international best sellers translated into more than 18 languages. Neither Miep nor Hannah had been willing to tell their entire stories until meeting Alison. Also for young people, *A Special Fate*, about Chiune Sugihara, the little-known Japanese diplomat who saved 6,000 Jews and others during the war.

Among those who have singled her out as a protector and chronicler of Holocaust experiences has been Elie Wiesel, who said of her: "Let us give recognition to Alison Gold. Without her and her talent of persuasion, without her writer's talent, too, this poignant account, vibrating with humanity, would not have been written." Other works include the adult nonfiction book *Fiet's Vase and Other Stories of Survival, Europe 1939-1945*, 25 interviews with survivors. This work is her farewell to that subject matter and *Love in the Second* Act is her first nonfiction since then. She has also published a short work in the Cahier Series, American University of Paris/Sylph Editions "Lost and Found."

Her nonfiction work has received awards ranging from the Best of the Best Award given by the American Library Association, to a Merit of Educational Distinction Award by the ADL, and a Christopher Award for affirming the highest values of the human spirit, among others.

Alison Leslie Gold has published literary fiction including *Clairvoyant, The Imagined Life of Lucia Joyce.* Jay Parini said about it: "A vividly written book that plays daringly in the no-mans-land between biography and fiction." Her novel, *The Devil's Mistress* was nominated for the National Book Award and her latest novel, *The Woman Who Brought Matisse Back from the Dead*, was recently released. Additionally she has published two novellas, *The Potato Eater* and *Not Not a Jew*.

She divides her time between New York and an island in Greece.

***

Darin Elliott was initially born in the suburbs of San Jose, California. A second birth came at age 23 when Italian friends in Los Angeles (where he moved to get a University degree in Writing) took him to Italy, and he fell in love with Europe and with Travelling. He has pretty much been on the road ever since, all over Europe and India, stopping to settle in various spots on the earth to get to know other cultures and people and the human potential.

Parallel to the external movement was an internal one which passed through the territories of Religion, Philosophy, Metaphysics, Mythology, and finally, sitting alone and silent and still to pull all the fragments into a whole. Numerous articles on his philosophical inquiries were published in the UK journal 'New Humanity'.

At any given moment he resides in an old stone house in rural France or a castle in Bavaria or a cow-dung hut in the Himalayas or a mansion on the Thames River outside London, or any one of numerous other spots he considers home on the planet.

www.ingramcontent.com/pod-product-compliance
Lightning Source LLC
Chambersburg PA
CBHW061613170626
46811CB00001B/416